Robert Wallace

Tycoon of Crime: Phantom Detective Saga

OK Publishing 2021

Robert Wallace

Tycoon of Crime: Phantom Detective Saga

Published by

MUSAICUM

Books

- Advanced Digital Solutions & High-Quality book Formatting -

musaicumbooks@okpublishing.info

2021 OK Publishing

ISBN 978-80-272-7877-0

Contents

Chapter I
Maiden Flight

The lonely shack stood in the chill night gloom, its windows faint squares of light. Thin mist, driven by a wind which shook the dark branches of surrounding heavy trees, swirled coldly about the small, solitary building. Within it, under the glare of a single naked ceiling bulb, two men stood with their backs to the bolted oak door. They were watching a third man who crouched across the room before the gleaming dials of a small but full equipped short-wave radio apparatus.

His hands-slender, nervous hands-were turning the dials with swift, jerky motions. The back of his hatless head was a shiny black knob, plastered-down hair glistening like patent leather in the light. His slender, crouched body swayed as he worked, graceful except for its slight jerkiness. His flashy top-coat trailed on the boarded floor.

Harsh, raucous static coughed abruptly from a loudspeaker, rising and diminishing as the man turned the dials.

"What's the matter, Slick? Can'tcha get it?" came the coarse, deep voice of one of the two, a huge, barrel-chested hulk of a man who seemed almost to fill the cramped little shack. His fedora hat seemed pygmy-sized over his wide, swart face with its small, glinting eyes, flattened nose, and wide gash of mouth.

He took a step forward as he spoke, moving with a loping, almost simian gait, one arm swinging at his side, the other nestled with snug ease around a blue steel Thompson submachine gun.

"Me," he snarled, "I'm gettin' tired of waitin' around here like this."

"Shut up!"

The authoritative command came in a harsh, jerky staccato from the man at the radio. He turned from the set. The light fell on his face-olive skinned, its darkly handsome features marred by a livid, zigzag scar which ran across his left cheek from chin to ear.

"I'll get it any minute now if you keep quiet."

He turned to the third man who was standing immobile as a statue, a faint wisp of smoke from the cigarette in his lips alone giving him semblance of movement. Tall, lean, he had an angular face with pale, expressionless eyes.

"Luke!" he snapped. "You sure you tipped off the others?"

Without moving the man Luke answered: "They'll be around on the dot, Slick."

The patent-leather hair of the man called Slick showed again as once more he bent to the dials. The static continued, grating in the silent shack.

Then, suddenly, Slick's crouching figure tensed as through the cloud of that static a voice began to materialize.

"Listen, guys!"

Slick turned the dials more. The static diminished, the voice grew in volume and clarity. A crisp, incisive voice speaking rapidly, with clear enunciation.

"—Plane Number One from Chicago, calling Newark Airport-Pat Bentley, pilot, speaking-Plane Number One —"

Out of the night, out of the dark ether, came that call. And as the three men in the shack listened with tense interest, there was a swift answering voice.

"Newark Airport. Go ahead, Bentley."

"We're still over the Pennsylvania, nearing Balesville. Visibility getting bad up here at fifteen thousand. Been keeping altitude to cross the Alleghenies and to get best speed, but clouds are too thick. Don't worry, though. We're smack on the radio beam. Ought to make Newark in another hour."

Slick rose to his feet. His dark eyes glinted, and there was a crooked, evil smile on his lips as he looked at his two companions.

"Newark in another hour, eh?" he chortled. "That's what he thinks!"

"Number One going off," said the voice in the loudspeaker. "I'm taking the controls again. Stand by."

Slick glanced at his wrist-watch. His slender body had gone tense again.

"We've got to be all set, guys! Luke-you keep your ears on that radio. Ape, you just keep that mug of yours closed."

The burly man with the tommy gun at once broke that command.

"Listen," came his coarse-toned protest, and there was a baffled look in his small, wide-set eyes. "I don't savvy this business, honest! What are we gonna do? I thought we was bein' paid to mess around with that railroad-wreckin' them trains an' —"

"If you was bein' paid to think, you'd sure be out of luck!" Slick cut in with his harsh staccato. "Stop worryin'. The guy who gives us our orders knows his stuff, an' I don't mean maybe. You ain't workin' for no mobster, punk. You're workin' for the Tycoon!"

Awe threaded his voice as he pronounced that title-and the awe communicated itself at once to the burly Ape, who winced and was silent. Luke remained immobile, but the dangling cigarette in his thin lips bobbed slightly, as if to express his own feeling of respect.

"Yes, an' the Tycoon knows his stuff," repeated Slick. "Maybe it's the swag on that plane." His eyes narrowed. "But I ain't trying to figure it. Whatever it is, it's gonna put dough in our pockets."

He broke off as once more the loudspeaker came to life.

"Pat Bentley calling-Visibility worse —I think I'll go down a ways —"

"He thinks he'll go down," Luke echoed, his words significant despite his expressionless tone.

"Yeah." Slick's malignant smile flickered again. "He don't know the half of it!" He moved hurriedly across the floor. "Got to be ready now! Any minute the time'll come. Any minute!"

* * *

Through the high-swirling cloud banks piled seemingly against the very stars, the huge-winged Douglas transport sliced downward, twin motors thundering, propellers churning the mists.

At times those mists swallowed the big plane completely. Then it would reappear, a great, silvery, birdlike shape, with lights showing from its cabin, and green and red running lights on its wing tips.

Below, through gaps in the mist, mountains showed dark, jutting peaks, gaping valleys. Presently, as the heavier clouds were left drifting above, the big monoplane leveled in its flight, straightened to roar ahead.

In the cozy, lighted cabin, ultramodern in its appointments, the dozen passengers gratefully unstrapped the belts they had been cautioned to fasten during the descent. They settled back comfortably, secure in the knowledge that this plane was in capable hands, and that even through mist the invisible but complicated network of radios and beacons which had made sky-travel as fully developed as any railroad on signal-marked tracks, helped guide the ship safely through the night.

"Coffee?"

A trim-uniformed stewardess, her cap set jauntily over her copper-tinted hair, emerged from her compartment to pass down the corridor with her tray. She was pretty in an efficient, capable-looking way. As if she regarded all the passengers as helpless patients as long as they were in the air, she treated them with firm solicitude.

"Now, Madame —" She was speaking to the rather stout but mink-coated wife of a big Chicago business man, who had fought for tickets on this first, new run of the airline. "—do take coffee. It will steady your nerves."

She passed the cup over, continuing her journey. Most of the passengers were men-men of wealth and position.

Two had brought wives; another a daughter. The cabin had the air of an exclusive, privileged society.

But not all of its occupants were so comfortably blase. In Seat Number 1, directly behind the closed-off pilot's compartment, a thin man in a black Homburg hat leaned out across the aisle. He had a scrawny, pallid face, its leanness accentuated by the tension that etched it. The cords of his neck stood out like whipcord. His eyes, in which all the personality of the man seemed concentrated, were dark, burning. He clutched a black briefcase in his arm as he spoke.

"I tell you, Garth, I feel nervous," came his low whisper, lost in the vibration of the motors. "Why did you insist on our taking this plane?"

Max Garth, a chunky man, muffled in a great-coat, from which his hatless head, large, square, and with a shock of greying, reddish hair spoke without leaning from the opposite seat. He wore thick-lensed glasses which gave his eyes a hard, concentrated stare.

"Cool down, Truesdale!" His low voice had a hard, brittle terseness, as if emotions were something he neither understood nor tolerated. Those who knew Max Garth-and he was famous in his profession of geology-knew him to be one of those cold men of science whose brains work only in cold logic, without sentiment. "You know it was a break-getting on this plane! Now nothing can go wrong. The whole affair will turn out as we expected. Why, the trip's almost over." He was reasoning as if with a child. "What is there to worry about?"

And like a child, David Truesdale relaxed a trifle. He, too, was a scientist: one of the country's foremost mining engineers, who had done noteworthy work in ventilating mines. But his work had become a shell into which he retired from worldly life, and he displayed that naivete which is so bewildering in men otherwise brilliant.

"Guess you're right, Garth. It's just nerves." He passed a blue-veined hand nervously over his pallid face.

"And don't hug that briefcase so," Garth said sourly. "Maybe you'd better give it to me!" His voice had an edge in it as it dropped still lower. "You don't want to attract attention."

Truesdale's clutch tightened on the briefcase as these words seemed instantly to bring back his fear. His eyes were burning, bright. "What's the use?" he began fearfully. "If someone knows-and he must know —"

"Are you going to bring up those threats again?" Garth's glasses seemed to glare. "Are you going to take the phone call of some crank seriously?"

"But if you had heard that voice over the phone!" Truesdale said shakily.

"I did," Garth returned coolly.

"What?" The eyes of David Truesdale went wide. "You mean, he-he threatened you too, this person who calls himself—" His voice was a frightened whisper. " —the Tycoon?"

Garth stiffened a little at that title; but his voice was contemptuous.

"Yes," he conceded. "He called. And gave me the same time limit. Nine o'clock tonight."

"But you never said a word about it."

"Because there's nothing to say, except to the police, when we get to New York."

Abruptly Garth broke off. He had turned in his seat, and his glare-glassed eyes caught sudden sight of pretty Nancy Clay, the stewardess, standing directly behind the two seats with her coffee tray. She was staring at them both, her lips half parted.

Garth darted a warning look at Truesdale who seemed oblivious of her presence. He spoke to Truesdale in a tone momentarily harsh:

"Well, forget about it! It's all a joke of no importance."

But the stark, haunted fear in Truesdale's eyes did not lessen. He started to speak again, then gulped and shut his lips tightly. Only then did he seem to become aware of the stewardess, as she came forward.

"Coffee, gentlemen?"

Garth shook his head. Truesdale growled a shaky: "No thank you, Miss."

"Come, come," she insisted. "It will warm you up. Make you feel fit for the landing."

"When do we land, stewardess?" Garth demanded.

She flicked around the wrist of the hand gripping the tray to look at her watch.

"Little more than three-quarters of an hour now," she said. "We're scheduled to land at nine-forty-five. It's now exactly two minutes to nine." She smiled, glancing at the closed partition in front of the two seats. "And if I know our pilot, we'll make that schedule!"

On the other side of the partition, his strong young hands gripping the Dep-wheel, Pat Bentley turned to his co-pilot.

"You can take over soon, Bill. I want to tell Newark now that everything's okay."

His eyes glanced through the oblique windows in the nose of the ship, at the dim mountains growing less precipitous ahead and below. Visibility was fairly good now. Not far ahead, Bentley saw the Balesville beacon funneling upwards, blinking like a white tentacle in the sky.

Yet, in the light from the myriad-instrumented dashboard, the young ace pilot's rugged, wind-swept face was etched tense. His broad shoulders were braced as if against some invisible foe. Veteran of thousands of flying hours, the big Douglas was a placid baby in his skilled hands-and yet, somehow, he did not feel right tonight.

A grim responsibility weighed him down. This was a maiden flight-for a big airline. Important people were in this plane; and there was important cargo too. Bentley had seen the armored truck come up on the Chicago field, seen the strong boxes being loaded into the great plane. Exactly what they contained he didn't know. But he did know he was carrying a fortune of some kind.

His keen eyes narrowed, thinking about the passengers. Two of them had acted queerly when they went aboard. The pilot had overheard a few words, tense words. Now that he thought of it, he realized that was what had created the uneasiness in him.

Garth and Truesdale. Two big scientists. Working, just now, Bentley knew for the Empire and Southwest Railway line. He grinned crookedly. That railway was in a slump: the growth of airline travel hadn't helped it any-Why had Truesdale looked so frightened when he climbed into the plane?

And why had Garth looked so icily cold?

Bentley cursed himself inwardly. He well knew just what part of his nature made him so curious about things like this. Once a newspaper man —

Yes, he had worked for a paper, a big New York paper. For several years he had been a flying reporter, and a radio news commentator. His voice had become as famous for its rapid-fire reports as Floyd Gibbons. He had covered many "exclusives," but now his real love, flying, had claimed him again and he had welcomed the job of piloting this new transport.

"It's just nine, Pat. Better call in Newark." The voice of the young co-pilot held the proper amount of respect for his "skipper."

"Right!" Quickly Pat Bentley snapped out of his reverie. "Take her, Bill." And added, listening to the neutral sound of the radio compass. "She's right smack on the beam now."

He released the Dep-wheel and rudder bars in precise synchronization with the moment that his co-pilot took them in control. Adjusting earphones under his trim visor-cap, he picked up the radio microphone.

" —Number One calling Newark-Number One calling Newark."

"This is Newark," came the prompt answer. "Go ahead, Number One."

"We're passing Balesville now. Visibility okay at eight thousand. How's the weather ahead?"

"Ceiling nine thousand. Visibility good."

"We may still beat the schedule," Bentley stated, hopefully, then broke off.

A buzzer had sounded in the little glass-windowed compartment in the nose of the big ship. It rang once, then again-imperatively. The co-pilot jerked up his head.

"Someone ringing, Pat."

"Just a minute," Bentley clipped into the microphone.

He reached back with annoyance, to unlock the partition door. And then his annoyance changed to sudden surprise.

His eyes went wide, stark, with horrified amazement!

Chapter II
One Did Not Die

"Just a minute."

In the modernistic, gleaming radio cupola of Newark Airport, those words of Pat Bentley's had emanated from the loudspeaker.

Two uniformed operators sat at tables in the brightly lighted room, handling two microphones. Two more stood at the big sets, with earphones glued on, their eyes watching the great, humming transmitters, the many tubes and condensers. From this room planes in the sky and on the field were guided; and though the atmosphere was tense, the work was performed with smooth efficiency.

Tonight, attention had been focused chiefly on the new flight from Chicago. While no other planes had been neglected, the men in the airport cupola had given their utmost cooperation to the big Douglas to see that the trip was smooth and successful.

The confident, incisive voice of Bentley had kept them reassured, even when the Douglas had been flying in the high clouds of fog. They had followed its every move, knew the exact position with which it should correspond with the big map on the wall.

As Bentley's voice said "Just a moment," the radio man at the microphone who had conducted the conversation with the plane relaxed, smiling.

"Two to one he beats the schedule!" he offered, and had no comers. "This is going to boost the Harvey Airlines all right. It's the fastest Chicago run in the air! And with Bentley the safest —"

He broke off, suddenly jerking up his head. From the loudspeaker came a low exclamation. Then —

"Wait!" Bentley's voice, no longer crisp but suddenly sharp, agitated. "Something's the matter! Something's wrong!"

The four men in the room stiffened, their confidence changing to quick alarm. The man at the microphone jerked forward.

"What's the matter, Bentley?" he snapped. "What —"

Then it came!

Of a sudden the loudspeaker seemed to burst into a din of raucous sound, which filled the cupola and brought a cry of alarm from every throat.

The first sound was like some rumbling detonation, brief yet reverberating. It was followed by a terrible, rending crackle! Horrified, the men in the cupola froze into rigid immobility, aware that something dreadful had just happened out in the night sky. And then, curdling their blood, came the hoarse scream:

"She's burning! She's burning!"

Pat Bentley had screamed those ghastly words! Screamed them more, it seemed, with horrified amazement than fright. Screamed them above that horrible, crackling roar.

"Fire!" Bentley shrieked, "It's broken out! The whole ship's burning like so much paper!"

"Bentley!" Helpless, the radio operator was wringing his hands at the microphone. "Good God, Bentley, what are you saying? What —"

The dreadful sounds from the night grew to a crescendo in the loud speaker. The crackling roar filled the room, And now, faint but horrifying, came other sounds-human cries. Cries of terror, of panic, of agony.

"God, she's going down! She's going to crash!" Bentley's frenzied voice came again. "The fire's creeping up —I can feel the heat-getting worse-worse! No hope! Going to crash —"

Abruptly the voice and the sounds ceased.

The radio went dead. In that awful moment, the aviation men's eyes showed the vivid horror of their air-trained imaginations. As if they could see a flaming Douglas plane, crashing like a fiery torch somewhere out in the night miles away. The fire consuming it, its radio crumpling, its passengers and its pilot caught helpless, without a chance of escape!

Then came swift reaction. The radio men hurled into a simultaneous rush of action. All other work was momentarily suspended. Both microphones carried frantic messages as their operators spoke in rapid fire.

"Trenton! Calling Trenton! Any more signals from Number One?"

"Balesville, Pennsylvania! Any reports of Number One in that vicinity?"

One of the operators picked up a phone. "Hangar Five! Send out planes to locate Number One!" He gave details, then: "Get me the commanding officer of Miller Field-Hello! Can you send out some flyers to aid in reported burning of transport?"

The continued calls set into motion every available machinery. As always, an air disaster brought swift cooperation from the Army Air Force, as well as from all commercial units.

The chief operator, having set such machinery in motion, spoke with gripping tension.

"We've got to get hold of Mr. Harvey! He must be informed of this at once. What a ghastly blow to the new line!"

Even as he spoke, out in the night, scores of searching planes were already taking the air. The hunt for the huge transport which had disappeared in the night was in full, feverish swing —

* * *

And meanwhile, outside a small shack rearing near heavy, wind-swaying trees, a group of shifting, shadowy figures, most of them in slouch hats with low-pulled brims, were gathering tensely.

There was a stench in the air —a burning, smoking stench. There was a dying, ruddy glow which flickered over coarse faces, over malignant, furtive eyes.

But the eyes of the group were all drawn hypnotically to a small closed coupe which had just emerged out of the night, come to a stop before them.

At first glance that coupe looked like the usual model of a well-known high-priced make of car. But closer inspection would have revealed the unusual heaviness of its metal body, the thickness of its glass windows. The window opposite the tense, dark figures was not quite completely closed; a crack showed on top. But glass protected the head of the car's lone occupant.

A face looked out through that glass —a strange, grotesquerie of a face whose features seemed to shimmer as if made of jelly. It was a ghastly sight, even though the men watching knew it was caused by some imperfection in the thick, bullet-proof glass.

Impossible to tell the true features of that distorted face. It remained, by virtue of the glass, a vague blur; frightening, yet malignantly compelling.

"And so everything has come off exactly as I planned!"

The voice came from the crack of the coupe's window. It was a ghastly voice, a sort of harsh whisper which eddied out into the silent night. It spoke in blighting malice.

"It has gone off like clockwork! And they will hunt in vain for the wreck! I commend you-all of you! Especially you three who were in the shack."

Slick, his head a dark shiny knob in the night, stepped forward with his nimble, jerky grace. Ape, still gripping the blue-steel tommy gun, stood grinning, while the man named Luke quietly lit a new cigarette.

"Hell, it was a cinch, Boss!" Slick spoke towards the car. "You had it figgered just right!"

An eerie chuckle sounded from the coupe, as the distorted face shimmered behind the glass.

"I always have things figured! And now we must prepare for my next enterprise! My work has only begun. The night is still young, and by midnight I strike again-this time in New York! There another enemy, perhaps even two, will pay for opposing me!" Harshly the whisper rose, with fanatical triumph. "Soon everyone will know the power of the Tycoon!

"And you, who are only one part of my mob, will see that you are not working for any small stakes. Before I am through, there will be millions-millions!" He repeated that word with avaricious greed which swiftly communicated itself to his listeners, to show in their evil faces. "Just obey my orders and nothing can stop us! Midnight tonight-remember, that is the time I have set. And I want you all to check your watches and synchronize them with my own now."

Watches came out or were turned up on wrists. The Tycoon gave the minute, and the watches were set.

"At midnight then," came the eerie voice. It lowered, giving further orders. Then the self-starter of the coupe whined; the engine purred.

"So I will go. And you will all hurry, too. I trust you checked up, as I said-on the dead?" he pronounced the phrase with grim mirth. "Did you take all the effects of Truesdale and Garth?" Hate threaded his tone as those names were spoken. There were gruff assents. "Good! And the pilot? You made sure of the pilot?"

As he spoke eyes shifted to the ruddy, dying glow. A few faces paled a little sickly.

"Yeah, I made sure he's dead," a squatly-built man stepped forward to answer. The ruddy glow revealed his squarish head, set low on wide shoulders. His face was crooked-featured, as if one-half of it had slid beneath the other. "I seen his brass buttons."

"You mean," the Tycoon said bitingly, "that there were two such men with brass buttons, don't you, Maxie? There was a co-pilot too."

Maxie's crooked face showed surprise. "But there was only one, Boss. I —"

"You bungling fool." The whisper lashed out like a whip, in sudden, frenzied rage. "Slick, count those bodies! Tell me the count!"

Slick hurried forward. He was quick to return with an answering number, but when he told it a snarl of enraged conviction came from the coupe.

"It's true then! One of them escaped! He's loose! That must be Bentley, the pilot, from what I know of his stubborn character. But he can't be far! He must be found-he must be killed!" The voice fairly crackled. "He must die before he can menace my plans!"

His fierce words lashed the whole crowd to action. Automatics glinted as they were whipped out. Ape gripped his tommy gun. Breaking up into smaller groups, thugs were scouring the vicinity-with murder in their eyes.

"He can't escape!" The voice of the Tycoon spurred them on. "There is only one way he could have headed. Get him! Get him no matter how far you have to follow him!"

* * *

Yes, Pat Bentley was alive!

He was disheveled, his face smoke-blackened, his eyes wild with horror and shock-but he was very much alive as he ran furtively through a sleepy little village-the village of Mulford, New York. A long, long way from where he had last radioed a message from his doomed plane.

His brain was a rioting tumult of rage, of horror, of anguished realization. Now he knew the reason for all his presentiments. And those two men he had felt queerly about at the outset of the flight. Garth and Truesdale.

He knew now the meaning of the frightened words he had heard in their conversation. But what about those strong boxes on the plane? Had they melted, burned? Their valuable unknown contents been destroyed? Conjectures raced through his mind as the question rose: What to do!

Then his wild eyes caught the light window of an all-night drug store. A telephone!

The lone clerk on duty in the store was dozing in a corner and did not even see Bentley. The disheveled, smoke-blackened pilot lurched across the floor to a single booth. His eyes glanced wildly around, then he entered, closing the door, change jangling as his hand reached into his pockets.

"Long-distance-New York City —" his voice came in a gasping croak. "I want New York City Police Headquarters. The number is Spring Seven Three One Hundred. Hurry-emergency!"

He was crazily putting in coins as he spoke, the toll-bells clanging. The urgency of his voice evidently brought swift cooperation from the telephone office.

The connection was made.

"Police Headquarters," boomed a stentorian voice.

"Let me speak to the commissioner: This is a matter of life and death. I've important information."

There was a pause at the other end. Faint words there; then a click of switches.

"Hello!" came a gruff voice. "This is Chief Deputy Inspector Gregg. Who's calling?"

"I want the commissioner."

"You can tell me what you have to say. I'm in charge of the Detective Division." And the man on the New York end of the line repeated: "Who's calling?"

"Listen!" Again Bentley ignored the question. His voice came rapid-fire, with crisp incisiveness, with the clear yet rapid enunciation that had made him famous as a news commentator. "Something's going to happen in New York at midnight at Grand Central! A murder —a devilish murder! There's a fiend behind it! I heard him talking! You police must stop him! You must —"

Abruptly Pat Bentley whirled. Was that a movement outside the drug store? Or just a shadow? The voice of the Manhattan inspector was barking questions in the receiver-but suddenly reaching a new decision, Bentley hung up without another word, without telling who he was.

He sneaked across the floor past the dozing clerk, glancing out. No one in sight. His imagination? Or perhaps a premonition. For the trail he had left would be wide open. They'd be after him.

He had done what had to be done immediately. Even as he had been talking he had realized he could not chance further information to any phone, nor tell what he knew to any police inspector. He must get to New York City, in person. He had phoned because he knew that not even a miracle could get him there before midnight, and at least he had warned the police, though they had no idea whose murder they were to prevent or who had given the information. But now —

As he hurried through the dark village streets, Bentley's eyes gleamed; those far-sighted eyes of the born flyer. There was one man to whom he could tell the whole ghastly story-the incredible story. The man who had been his boss when he was a newspaperman. Frank Havens, owner of the New York *Clarion*!

Havens would know what to do with this dynamite news that would be too inflammable for the police! For Havens knew how to contact the one person who could cope with such a thing; the great unknown detective who had unraveled other baffling and bloody enigmas.

"*The Phantom!*" Bentley's dry lips whispered, as they twisted in a crooked grin of hope. "The Phantom-must be-called!"

Chapter III
Murder on the Balcony

Night in Manhattan. In Times Square, the city was wide awake and gay, the bright lights glaring. Crowds from the theaters were hurrying to nightclubs and restaurants. From the waterfront fog-horns tooted, factories still ground out their work, smoke belching from their chimneys. To the east, cars streamed like illuminated, linked chains across the bridges.

Other cars streamed west, too, to enter the Holland Tunnel, to whisk over the George Washington Bridge. There were but few lonely streets in the teeming metropolis.

Wall Street and the surrounding financial district were deserted, the office buildings rising like dark canyon walls. But its streets were still pounded by alert patrolmen.

The poverty-stricken tenement sections where evil figures stalked-drunks and derelicts, shifty underworld characters-also lay in sleepy gloom. And police were watchful, knowing that no night passed in these districts without some violence and bloodshed.

Police Inspector Thomas Gregg's bulking form sat in the cushioned shield-bearing limousine which was whisking him and a hard-eyed subordinate uptown, toward Grand Central, its short-wave radio bringing every police call that went out from Headquarters.

"I suppose that anonymous call from Mulford, New York, was from a crank," the inspector grumbled "But I guess it's just as well not to take chances. That voice I heard on the phone-There was something about it-something familiar. Kinda made me sure feel the tip was hot!" He pulled out his watch. "Pretty close to midnight. Get on up to Grand Central. If anybody thinks he's going to pull any murder there —"

* * *

In a huge, brightly lighted room six tense men sat at a long conference table, talking in low voices as they watched a wall-clock which showed that the hour of midnight was approaching.

A more diverse-looking group could not have been found. Yet these six men were all linked by mutual reputations in the field of science and engineering. All were famous throughout the country for their work in these lines.

Nor was that all that linked them.

There was another bond which seemed to hold them together as with some hidden magnet. A strange, furtive bond-one of conflicting fear and hope.

Near the unoccupied head of the table Vincent Brooks, one of the country's leading electrical engineers, ran a gaunt hand over his long, rugged face, his dark, hard eyes narrowing beneath beetling brows.

Next to him a wiry man with a shock of grey hair that kept getting into his eyes, hunched tensely forward. Leland Sprague, a surveyor.

Beside those two sat Joseph Ware and Paul Talbert. Ware was a quiet, well-built, grey-haired man who was a specialist in waterways and dams. Paul Talbert, a shoring engineer, was broad-shouldered, with a wind-burned face, a military mustache, blond hair and clear, far-seeing eyes.

The fifth man of the group, solid-built but pallid-faced, with crow's-feet under his eyes, toyed nervously with a pencil. He was a geologist named Donald Vaughan.

Finally, running his hand over his high, thin-haired skull, was John Eldridge, another surveyor.

"Well, gentlemen?" Paul Talbert spoke, sitting erect, his mustache bristling. "I still say the time is opportune! Everything has worked out as we planned it! We have only to go ahead." His eyes gleamed.

"What about the threats?" Joseph Ware demurred. The quiet-looking waterways man's voice was low and tense, and only his eyes showed the panic he kept from his quiet face, "Remember, I've been getting them. And now that we've learned what happened to Truesdale and Garth —"

"You're jumping to conclusions, Ware!" Sprague broke in, a little shrilly, pushing back his shock of grey hair. "They haven't found that plane yet! We don't know for sure."

"Besides, it was undoubtedly an accident, that disaster!"

"Undoubtedly." Talbert agreed. "And while it means a delay, we can still go ahead as we planned! This is no time for faint heartedness! Don't forget what's in this for all of us if it works out!"

There was a slight stir around the table. Greed, that dark driving urge which at times can overcome the best of men, flashed in several eyes. Greed-and fear!

"I agree with Talbert!" Vincent Brooks, the rugged-faced electrical engineer, clipped. He laughed harshly. "And I have been warned myself by these strange phone messages! But whoever this Tycoon is, he can't know our secret. Only we know it at this present moment! And no one but ourselves will ever know it fully!"

"Lord, if it ever leaked out!" Donald Vaughan strained forward, the crows-feet twitching under his eyes. "If this Tycoon suspected it he could ruin us all!" He shook his head. "And if the Government ever knew —"

He broke off abruptly, as if not daring to finish. And again the current of invisible fear coursed about the table.

"We've got to keep our heads!" Eldridge said, his thin-haired head bobbing. "We're in this thing together no matter what happens."

Like an invisible curtain a hush closed down on the group. Lips clamped suddenly tight. Eyes hid the emotions which a moment before had shown stark and clear.

The frosted glass door leading from an anteroom had opened unceremoniously. Three more men came in.

The one in advance, a heavy-set man, florid of face, his head bald save for a fringe of iron-grey hair, strode toward the table.

"Good evening, gentlemen! Glad to see all of you got here early. I hope you have made yourselves at home here in our executive office."

In the sudden silence, the six scientists heard the muffled but continuous bustle of sound outside the offices; the movement of hundreds of feet; and, further away, an occasional clang of bells, a hiss of air-brakes.

This big room, the New York office of the Empire and Southwest Railway, was situated on the gallery floor of Manhattan's biggest railway terminal, the Grand Central, famous throughout a continent.

Talbert was the first to speak, in a quiet, hard voice, to the rugged man who had strode forward.

"Hello, Strickland! We've been waiting for you!"

James Strickland, vice-president of the Empire and Southwest Railway, moved to the head of the table and took the chair there.

The second newcomer, Charles Jenson, secretary of the railway company, a thin-haired, bespectacled man with a mild, timid manner, also joined the gathering.

And if these two high railway officials seemed almost like aliens in the conclave of scientists, the third man who had entered at their heels was out of place with both groups.

He stood alone near the door —a big, broad man with grizzled, grey-peppered hair. A man who gave the impression of dominant strength.

"Oh, sit down, Mr. Harvey!" Strickland said to him, gesturing as if just remembering the amenities. "You gentlemen must know Mr. Andrew Harvey, president of the Harvey Airlines!"

Tensing again, the eyes of the six scientists swiveled to the visitor.

He grinned —a hard, tight grin-meeting their glances levelly.

"I'll stand," he said in a booming voice. "What I have to say won't take long. I'm here on business-cold, plain business! I'm here to make a cash offer for this railway! While Strickland and Jenson have given me little encouragement, I thought I might find the rest of you more interested!"

No electric shock could have caused a more startled reaction. Their eyes widening, for a moment the six scientists seemed speechless.

Then Strickland spoke, as if for the startled men.

"This is most irregular, Mr. Harvey! In the absence of the line's president, Mr. Garrison, who as you know, is in St. Louis —"

"I'll deal with Garrison when he gets back!" Andrew Harvey snapped. "Right now I'm dealing with all of you here. That's enough!"

A mirthless smile curved Talbert's lips beneath his mustache. "You seem to be laboring under a misconception, Mr. Harvey," he said. "We are merely technicians working for the Empire and Southwest Railway."

Harvey's laugh was harsh, contemptuous. "You're wasting your breath! I know you're the chief stockholders of this railroad, all of you! You've all acquired big blocks of shares! And I'm here to buy you out-to take those shares at better than their present market value!"

The silence was ominous. The six men, rigid now, turned fierce glances to Strickland and Jenson. Strickland blurted something. The mild Jenson spoke in a meek voice.

"I'm sure Mr. Harvey didn't learn that from us." The secretary's tone was conciliating. "These things leak out, you know."

"I make it my business to know such things!" Harvey said shortly. "And I know you men, with your technical skill, are trying to put this railway on its feet! But it isn't worth the effort. The only use for it now is if it can be run in conjunction, as an auxiliary, to my own airline! That's why I want it. If you think you can run it in competition, you're sadly mistaken!" His eyes narrowed to slits, his face grew grim. "Even the sabotaging of my new Chicago transport plane isn't going to cripple my growing airline!"

There was a gasped intake of breath; and indignant scrape of chairs.

Joseph Sprague, the wiry surveyor, was on his feet then, his shock of grey hair dancing.

"Are you daring to insinuate that we had any connection with that plane disaster?" he demanded shrilly.

"Take it that way if you want," said the blunt Harvey. His lips curled. "Of course, all of you will begin to produce alibis showing you were in New York City at the time of the disaster; but you men do get around, don't you? And there are more ways than one of cooking a goose, especially if you're a technician!"

Talbert leaped up. "If this is a joke, Harvey," he said with cold fury, "it's in pretty bad taste."

Sprague leaned forward, fuming.

"It's outrageous! I refuse to listen to it! You can have my answer to your offer right now, Mr. Harvey! I'll see you in Hell before I'll make any deal with you!"

For a moment it seemed he would spring bodily upon the weathered-faced airline president, smaller though he was. Instead, however, he pushed back his chair and, his face flaming, strode out of the conference room, slamming the door behind him.

Strickland's eyes showed haggard worry. "You shouldn't have said that, Harvey! After all, a knife can have two edges. Sprague was a close friend of both Truesdale and Garth-also of our company, and passengers on that plane. Truesdale and Garth were valuable men," he added significantly, "very valuable men."

"And also," Joseph Ware put in grimly, "don't forget that there has been a lot of sabotage of the railway itself. Especially in the Southwest."

It was the airline man's turn to stiffen indignantly. Glaring, he seemed about to voice an angry retort when Vincent Brooks, the gaunt electric wizard, suddenly rose to his feet, pointing at the clock-whose hands were converging to midnight!

"It's time for the new electric sign to go on!" Brooks announced. "Inasmuch as I constructed it, I'd like to be out there to see it!"

Strickland nodded hastily. "Of course. We all want to see it." He turned to Harvey. "You'll join us, Mr. Harvey? You noticed the preliminaries as you came in. Perhaps you'll be interested to see how modern we, too, can be in our methods."

The whole group were hurriedly rising. With a scowling Harvey accompanying them, they passed through an anteroom, emerged upon a gallery, then descended marble-bannistered steps which led them directly upon the immense, dome-ceilinged concourse.

An unusually large throng milled on the floor; a throng much larger than the usual flow of travelers who always streamed through the big terminal. Huge banners, all proclaiming A New Era in Railroading, gave the huge place a festive air.

Over the noise of the crowds sounded the blare of trumpeting music. A band composed of dusky Pullman porters in gaudy uniforms, led by a busby-hatted drum-major, was playing "Casey Jones."

"What is this anyhow?" Harvey snorted. "A circus in a railroad station?"

Strickland glared at him, but the mild-eyed secretary, Jensen, said, in an explanatory tone:

"In just one minute now, you will see that sign go on." With a moving forefinger he signified a continuous dark oblong strip of metal, dotted with electric bulbs, which ran around the four walls of the great concourse. "In St. Louis, Mr. Garrison, our president, will press a button. The impulse will be carried over our own wires to the device on the gallery which operates the sign."

"Very elaborate!" sneered Harvey. "But nothing can put this line on its feet, I'm warning you."

Nevertheless, he displayed interest as the Pullman band ended its number with a martial roll of drums. An expectant hush fell over the crowd. All eyes went to the strip of dark bulbs.

A second went by, then —

Abruptly, a flickering blaze of light leaped into life at the beginning of the strip, coursed jaggedly along the sign, forming bold letters-words:

GREETINGS TO THE PUBLIC-WE TAKE PLEASURE IN ANNOUNCING OUR MODERNIZED RAILROAD POLICY-OUR MANY NEW INNOVATIONS —

The words, with their smooth advertising, continued. The crowd watched.

—AND NOW IT IS TIME FOR THE MESSAGE OF THE TYCOON OF CRIME —

So smoothly did these words follow on the wake of the others that at first their utter strangeness was unnoticed by the crowd. But instantly sharply indrawn breaths of amazement issued from the group of men who had rushed down from the executive offices. Their eyes bulged as they followed those bold words, carried unerringly around the strip of bulbs.

—THE TYCOON OF CRIME HEREBY WARNS ALL THOSE WHO HAVE FLOUTED HIM —

The crowd had begun to murmur, to laugh as if believing this some deliberately humorous part of the ballyhoo, not yet understood.

"What's the meaning of those crazy words?" Strickland burst out.

"Meaning?" screamed a voice. "Good Lord, don't you realize? The Tycoon! The criminal we all laughed at!"

No one had noticed that Leland Sprague, the shock-haired surveyor who had so angrily left the conference room, had joined them. It was he who had made this outburst. His agitation seemed to have driven away all remembrance of his anger; his face was ashen. Madly he waved towards the coursing, illuminated words.

"The sign!" he choked. "He must have got at the box that makes the sign go!"

But while Jenson and Harvey both looked as bewildered as Strickland, the scientists in the group had all jerked rigid, their faces blanching.

Even the hard-featured Paul Talbert looked shaken.

Then Vincent Brooks, who had made the sign, suddenly dashed toward the gallery stair. John Eldridge, the thin-haired surveyor, also broke away at a run.

The bold words which thousands read continued to leap into view, and run around the sign like letters of fire.

—SOME HAVE LEARNED THIS VERY NIGHT OF MY POWER-OTHERS WILL SOON LEARN-MORE BLOOD WILL BE SPILLED-MORE WILL DIE-TAKE THIS LAST WARNING—

The explosion was deafening!

It crashed thunderously in the spacious interior of the dome-ceilinged concourse, the sheer concussion hurling many of the gaping crowd off balance.

From the center of the balcony, above the coursing sign, had leaped a blinding, hissing sheet of flame! The sign went dark even as the detonation followed. And at the same instant —

A scream of horror burst from scores of throats as, whisked off the balcony like some mere feather, a human shape came hurtling straight down —a shape of limp but flailing arms and legs.

That the body didn't fall on the panic-stricken crowd seemed sheer luck. With a ghastly thud it crashed to the tiled flooring beneath the balcony.

Strickland, Jenson, and the rest of their group rushed over as the din rose higher, though railway police were struggling to restore order.

They reached the inert heap on the floor, looked down. A scream broke from Charles Sprague, who pointed.

"It's Eldridge! Good God-Eldridge!"

John Eldridge was a gruesome sight. His body was a maimed, bloody heap which stained crimson the white-tiled floor. A whole portion of his chest had been blown out. A gaping hole showed the broken bones, ripped flesh, tatters of clothes. His face was frozen in a grimace of contorted agony, the eyes glazed and protruding like marbles.

Strickland cried out hoarsely. "And he was blown off the balcony-just when the sign went off! Where's Brooks? Brooks should know about the sign!"

His question was quickly answered by Donald Vaughan. The geologist had rushed up to the balcony, and his voice called down shakily. The rest hurried up there, oblivious that Andrew Harvey was no longer with them.

They found what was left of Vincent Brooks piled against the balcony wall. His head had almost been severed from his torso by the explosion. The chin was blown away, leaving a broken bulge of bloody jaw-bone. The features, bloated in death, were barely recognizable.

Opposite the corpse, on the stone balcony construction, was a shattered box of metal, its parts strewn about.

Strickland stared at it.

"That's where the strip that controlled the sign was running!" he burst out hoarsely. "It's blown to hell! This is ghastly-ghastly!"

Quick glances were shot up and down the balcony. It was empty. But the crowds from below, in mingled panic and morbid curiosity, were already surging up the stairs. Railway police fought them back. Then came the shrill whistles of regular city police on duty in this precinct.

And outside in the night, in the next moment, rose the scream of sirens.

The law was coming swiftly. And a certain shield-bearing limousine carrying a worried inspector was now hurtling straight to the terminal.

Chapter IV
The Corpse on the Pavement

Richard Curtis Van Loan, debonair young society man and *bon vivant,* turned his sixteen-cylin-dered Cadillac roadster onto upper Park Avenue and headed downtown through a neighbor-hood-which, in this section, was shabby and unkempt.

A slender, dark-haired girl in a pert, Buddhistic hat sat beside Van Loan, her dark, liquid eyes wistfully stealing now and then to his well-cut profile, etched in the dashboard lights.

In the spacious rumble seat, another couple sat, in each other's arms, and it could have been seen at a glance that they were newlyweds. The girl, blond and hatless, clung possessively to the young groom who had been one of the social register's most eligible bachelors until he had looked into her blue eyes.

"Say, where are you taking us, Dick?" the man suddenly leaned forward to ask.

"To my apartment," drawled Van Loan, without turning from the wheel, "where we will do justice, with champagne, to your marriage, then let you go off on your honeymoon in peace. Do you agree, Muriel?"

Muriel Havens smiled up at him.

"If you ask me, I have a sneaking suspicion the newlyweds are just dying to get rid of us!"

"Now Muriel!" the girl in the back protested. "We're not leaving until tomorrow. We even hoped to get your father's blessing before we went. Do you suppose we'll get a chance to see him?"

Muriel sighed. "I don't know. The paper's been keeping him pretty busy. He's in his office night and day."

"Isn't it extraordinary," Van Loan drawled languidly, "how some men will bury themselves in work? Why doesn't your dad let the *Clarion* run merrily along, Muriel, and step out for a good time?"

Muriel Havens's small but firm chin lifted. A momentary anger swept her eyes.

"Some people wouldn't understand it, I guess," she said pointedly. "But Dad feels he's doing something useful in this world."

Van Loan made a sad, clucking sound with his tongue.

"Ouch!" he said. "That remark has a vaguely personal tinge. But really, can you imagine me getting up the energy to indulge in hard labor?" He stifled a yawn.

On Muriel's lovely, intelligent face was disappointment. She could not have felt surprised.

Richard Curtis Van Loan was hardly a man of action. Good-natured, lazy, he fitted only into the social set, whiling away the hours with his select friends in pleasure and amusement. Because he was handsome and too wealthy for any one man, he was one whom doting mothers longed to have their daughters ensnare.

Yet, oddly, Muriel Havens had never accepted Van Loan as a mere lazy, social parasite, an idler who gayly flung to the winds the wealth his father had slaved to attain.

Again she glanced at the well-built young man beside her; at his strong hands, gripping the wheel with steady ease. And she shook her head, her lips pressed against any words of protest she might have felt like uttering.

As the roadster continued downtown the avenue changed in aspect. The shabby district suddenly gave way to Manhattan's most exclusive and wealthy residential section. They were riding down past the green-parked "islands" under which trains rumbled.

"Why so silent, Newlyweds?" Van drawled. "This is a celebration, not a funeral."

"Oh, don't mind us!" the young bridegroom laughed. "We're just sitting here smugly en-joying the idea of being married. And let me tell you, Dick, it's great! Why don't you try it sometime?"

"It is a thought," Van Loan grinned-and looked at Muriel Havens. For a moment, she saw in his eyes something that was seldom there; and so briefly now that she might have only imagined it. It was so totally out of gear with the languid, idling Van Loan.

Van saw her dark eyes glow-for that one moment. And turned back to the wheel, covering his expression with another suppressed ostentatious yawn.

Dick Van Loan knew Muriel was hurt by that gesture; wounded deeply. Yet it had been necessary. His hand had covered more than the yawn. It had covered an implacable bitterness which had tightened his lips and narrowed his eyes.

Had Muriel or the others had any inkling of the thoughts that were going through Van's brain at that instant, they would have been more than amazed.

They were stern, fierce thoughts. Thoughts sealed by a long-kept pledge within his mind. Thoughts that cruelly drove the human feelings of Dick Van Loan to some dull recess where he could only keep them for the distant future.

In his mind, Richard Van Loan was seeing vividly remembered sights, alien to his social life. He was seeing dark byways, where shadowy, evil figures stalked; he was seeing gruesome bodies, riddled, knifed, killed in other heinous fashions. He saw, too, the terrible implements of justice. The inexorable electric chair-the noose-the lethal chamber. And cowering, convicted criminals ensnared by them.

A grim parade of diabolical murderers who had thought they could cheat justice! Sometimes they had foiled the law, made a laughingstock of the police. But, like a relentless Nemesis, a single unknown had proved their undoing. The mysterious scourge of crime known as the Phantom Detective.

The Phantom! Throughout the world, in every law-enforcing agency, in Scotland Yard, in the *Surete,* to the Berlin Police that sobriquet had become a synonym of perfect crime detection. Just as, in the underworld, it had become a byword of fear and dread.

Richard Curtis Van Loan, sitting next to Muriel Havens, wished he could have turned to her now and driven the reproach and disappointment from her eyes by telling her the great secret. He wished he could have said:

> "Muriel, I am the Phantom Detective! Yes, I —Richard Curtis Van Loan, whom you hold in contempt and yet love. Your own father, Frank Havens, was responsible. It was he who told me years ago, that I was wasting my life and energy; he who suggested that I anonymously try to fight crime. Since then my life is no longer my own. I have to forego all that every normal man takes for granted as a part of his life. My lazy social life is just a pose-to enable me to gather energy for the next case, which can come at any moment. My real time is spent in study-the study of criminology, disguise, delving into realms you would never dream interest me. But perhaps some day, some time, when my case book is full, I can come to you, free and unshackled."

Aloud, however, Van Loan said with a lazy drawl as the car picked up speed, "Well, here we come. Now to negotiate a turn, get to the other side of the block-and home sweet home."

He did not look at Muriel Havens as he spoke, as he nodded toward the "island" beneath which sounded a dull rumble. The sidewalk opposite, dim in the street lights, was empty. On the corner toward the palatial apartment atop which was Van's luxurious penthouse residence. Van guided the purring roadster down to the intersection, thence around, waiting for the lights to make the complete turn before heading the car uptown on the other side of the block.

Steering towards the curb, he slowed the roadster. That was when his ever keen eyes-eyes trained to alertness by night as well as day-suddenly sharpened. Without giving thought to it, he had observed that the sidewalk had been empty as the roadster passed down the block, on the downtown side.

But now, coming up on this side, he saw that the pavement was no longer empty.

In the very middle of the block, a shadowy heap lay on the sidewalk.

A huddled, bulgy heap from which came no sign of movement.

"What is it, Dick?" Muriel had noticed his sudden stiffening.

Without replying, Van braked the roadster to an instant stop, apprehension tightening his lips.

Ignoring the questions of Muriel and the others, he slid quickly from behind the wheel, alighted in the street on his long legs, and hurried around the car to the sidewalk.

Only the dim light of the nearest street-lamp illuminated the bulgy heap.

But it was sufficient to bring out a gruesome sight.

The corpse of a well-built man lay at Van's feet. It lay half on its side, legs drawn up grotesquely to the stomach, hands clutching out like frozen claws.

The clothes of the man were so disheveled, torn, and begrimed with dirt and blood and what appeared to be soot, that they were scarcely distinguishable.

The man was hatless. His light-colored hair looked like a wet, flat mat-wet with crimson blood.

But it was to the face of the man, full of bruises that Van's eyes were drawn so grimly. Or rather, to what had once been a face.

On first glimpse it looked like some horrible smear of blood and dirt and torn flesh so that the outlines of the skull showed through. Near the lower right jaw was a huge, uneven hole; obviously made by a heavy-calibered bullet. Once, in Chicago, during a gang war, Van had seen a man shot in this fashion. Shot in the face at close range, so that the bullet had completely disfigured him.

Something of this face remained however. Though not enough to offer any clear picture. Grim-eyed, Van stared at the bloody, revolting face, at the glazed, blood-stained eyes which peered out stark and sightless. In the full moment he studied that face Van decided the man had been fairly young, had probably had well-formed features.

A gasped cry-he recognized Muriel Havens's voice-jerked him about. Quickly Van stepped around the corpse as he saw Muriel and the newlyweds standing, white-faced, on the pavement. With his tall, broad-shouldered figure he screened the gruesome corpse from them as best he could.

"Dick-that man! He's dead, isn't he?" In Muriel's choked-cry —a statement, rather than question, was horror.

"Yes, so it seems."

Van's languid drawl was slightly constricted. His mind was racing. Something was prodding it, hammering at it like some stray waif of memory trying to gain admittance.

"Better not come any closer," he said. "It's rather a nasty sight." He turned to the groom. "Listen. This has rather upset my night, but there's no sense in letting it spoil your party. Take my car, take Muriel with you. Continue your celebration without me. Just take the time to summon the first policeman you see and send him here. Better not tell him what's here or he might make you come back. I'll remain with-this."

Despite the fact that he still clung to his drawl, there was something so decisive and commanding in his manner that all three stared, unable to comprehend this change in the idle Van Loan. Again Muriel Havens's dark eyes swept to him with that strange, probing look: half hope, half unbelief.

She came forward, a brave look on her firm, finely chiseled features, "I'll stay here with you, Dick. Maybe I can help."

"Help? My dear girl, this is a matter for the police. I myself do not intend to stay any longer than I have to. Until the law takes over.

"By the way, don't mention my name when you call the policeman. I don't wish to be dragged into this. After the law comes, I shall discreetly retire; and because I feel a bit upset, take out a nice bottle to enjoy in solitude."

His drawl, forced back, was cold again. Once more Muriel's eyes went dull with disappointment and hurt.

But his words, as he had calculated, had the desired effect.

Chapter V
Clarion Call

Muriel Turned, gesturing to the others. In a moment they were piling back into Van's car, the bridegroom taking the wheel. Rolling from the curb, the big roadster moved up the avenue. Van caught a glimpse of Muriel Havens's white, hurt face, looking back through the darkness. But he thrust aside any emotion that face disturbed in him. For already his brain had turned into a cold, methodical machine, functioning in full power.

All languor had dropped from his athletic body. His movements had become dynamic, purposeful.

Again his gaze riveted to the mutilated face of the corpse on the sidewalk. Though the features were gone, there was something there that struck a reminiscent chord in the Phantom's brain. Something-what was it? What was that elusive identifying mark?

That vague memory in the back of his brain tugged at Van. He felt certain of one thing, however. Somewhere he had seen this man. But where? Under what circumstances?

He studied the clothes as his fingers swiftly searched through them. All the pockets were empty. Even the buttons of trousers and coat were missing. The material was blue serge, and though ripped, the suit still retained a certain trimness. A uniform, perhaps? Not a police uniform, but —

Then a sudden light flashed through Van's brain as he moved so that the street light fell more directly on the corpse. Though it was so deeply bloodied that at first it had not been distinguishable, the white streak in the dead man's hair was now plain to Van's keen, observant eyes. A peculiarly formed streak.

He had it! His eyes went narrow as his lips spoke a name.

"Pat Bentley!"

The young flyer who had once worked as a news commentator for Frank Havens!

In his role of idler, Van Loan had met Pat Bentley in the *Clarion* offices. He had noticed that streak in young Bentley's black hair, even as he had been admiring the nerve of the adventurous youngster. He had known then he would never forget that peculiarly distinguishing mark of the young flyer's. And Havens had told Van, later, that Bentley had become a crack transport pilot.

That blue serge material was used for the uniform of such a pilot. It plainly was a uniform, even though the telltale brass buttons were gone.

But-and bafflement came to Dick Van Loan's face-how had Bentley come to be killed in this horrible fashion here on Park Avenue?

Naturally Van did not know of the air disaster. It had occurred too recently, too far upstate, for any news of it to have reached farther than the newspaper offices yet, where the presses were even now whirling off the details of the air tragedy.

But he did know that finding Pat Bentley dead-killed in this vicious manner-and practically on his own doorstep, was a challenge to the Phantom, though there had been no such intention.

He had to find Pat Bentley's murderer!

He bent over the awful, mutilated face. The bullet, he saw, had entered the lower jaw, had come out behind the opposite ear. It had passed partially through the brain.

Death, then, would not have been instantaneous. A man might even live for awhile, manage to move for awhile, with such a wound.

Again he went through the clothes for some possible clue. This time he found something as his fingers turned back one of the trouser cuffs. Within it lay a few tiny bits of paper; like confetti.

Puzzled, Van straightened. Where had the dead man come from? The sidewalk had been empty when Van had driven past. No cars had passed before he had discovered the body, he was sure. His eyes scanned buildings, including his own apartment house. One of them, perhaps?

Suddenly his eyes sharpened, centering on the street itself. Little jagged smears of red showed on the concrete sidewalk, extending to the curb, out onto the asphalt of the street to the rail of one of the midstreet "islands." Blood! A brief trail of it.

The jigsaw-like clues clicked into place in Van's razor-sharp brain. The blood trail-the confetti-like bits in the trouser cuffs-the "island," beneath which he had heard a train rumbling a few minutes before his discovery of the corpse.

A train! That was the only possible answer. The "confetti" clinched it. The little paper bits were undoubtedly the punchings from a railway ticket.

That-and one other thing-clinched it. For as Van glanced toward the "island" he saw that the big iron ventilating grille in the center of the grass and shrubbery was undisturbed-but the smaller grille that usually covered the manhole-like square at one end of the "island" was off, tilted against the iron fence.

One of the workmen must have forgotten to replace it and bolt it from the under side. And Bentley had found the open grille. Some instinct must have guided him even in his blinded, mortally wounded condition.

Van's mind was racing. Pat Bentley, then, had been on a train, though in which direction it had passed Van couldn't tell. Doubtless the pilot had been shot on that train. Then he must have jumped, or fallen from it. The last ounce of his dying energy had been spent in climbing to the street level; getting as far as the Park Avenue sidewalk.

It was almost as if Fate had thrown Pat Bentley upon Van's doorstep, bringing him this case. For certainly Bentley could not have known that Van lived here, much less dreamed that Richard Van Loan was the Phantom! The fact that the man *had* fallen so near Van's own home was one of those bizarre coincidences at which the Phantom no longer scoffed.

Van prodded himself to haste. He must follow up his hunch-and quickly. There was need for haste otherwise, too, for glancing down the deserted block, he glimpsed a burly figure coming at a run, with a swinging night-stick. A beat patrolman. Muriel and the others must have sent him.

Richard Van Loan was in no mood to tarry and face inquiries now. His lithe body whisked into the dark shadow of building walls, streaking to the door of his apartment house.

No doorman was on duty at this late hour, and before the night elevator operator could see him, Van had slipped into his private elevator, closed its door, and pressed the starting button.

It took but a brief moment for him to reach his penthouse floor, high above the city. His key admitted him to his luxurious, French-windowed apartment. He strode through the foyer, into a living room, pressing on light-switches as he walked. Modernistic-globed lights flooded the place.

Flinging his coat to a chair, Van stepped beside a taboret on which stood two telephones and the phone directories. He flipped the Manhattan book open, found his number. Scooping up one phone he dialed swiftly.

"Grand Central Terminal Information," came a smooth, clerical voice.

Van's own voice was crisp, incisive; totally unlike his customary drawl.

"Will you tell me when the last train left from your terminal-and also the last train that arrived there?"

"Just a moment." The clerk, accustomed to answering even stranger questions, replied politely, yet with a certain tenseness of tone which made Van wonder. There seemed to be a lot of noise at that end of the wire, too, as if something were wrong.

Van was using one hand to get off his jacket, ripping open buttons of his shirt as the clerk's voice came again.

"Last train to depart was the Rochester Special. That was at eleven fifty. The last to arrive here was the Toledo Limited, at eleven thirty-eight."

Van glanced at his watch. It was twelve thirty-three now. Neither of those trains could be the right one. The run between the terminal and here was only a matter of some ten minutes either way.

"When is the next arriving train due?"

The answer brought a thrill of conviction to him.

"It's due now, sir. It's a few minutes late, but should be in any minute. The Buffalo Local-on Track Forty-one."

"Thanks!" Van hung up, eyes glittering.

That must be the train. Swiftly, he scooped up the second telephone.

This was a private line, one which connected him, as soon as he lifted the receiver, directly with the executive office of the New York *Clarion,* automatically causing the phone at that end to ring.

"Van!" The familiar voice of Frank Havens came instantly, a voice oddly threaded with gladness and surprise. "Why, I was just about to call *you!*"

"Listen, Frank!" Van spoke tersely, hurriedly. "I have no time to talk long! But I want you to use your influence to have a train, the Buffalo Local, due any minute at Grand Central Terminal, immediately searched by the railway and regular police. All passengers and crew to be held for the time being. No one is to be allowed to get away! It's important, Frank —I'll explain later. Can you do it quickly?"

"I can do it this instant!" came the reply, to Van's surprise. "As a matter of fact I have the railway officials on another wire even now! I was just about to call you after what they told me. But evidently you already know, though I don't see how —" the publisher broke off sharply. "I'll carry out your instructions-at once!"

"Good!" Van clipped, and hurriedly slammed down the hand-set, his ears echoing with Frank Havens's strange words!

So Havens had been about to call the Phantom-had railway officials on another wire. Certainly it could not be about this corpse Van had only moments ago discovered and identified. The train whence it had come was not yet in!

With conjectures whirling in his brain, Van was already hurrying into his bedroom now, closing the door behind him, turning the key in the lock for safety's sake. His shirt was off in a jiffy, his lithe arm muscles revealed in the bright light.

Quickly, he moved to a dressing table. In appearance it was a usual, though expensive piece of furniture. The maid who came in to clean had dusted it every day without suspecting that there was anything out of the ordinary about it, save perhaps the fact that, unlike most men's dressing tables, it had three extremely good mirrors.

Van pulled open a bottom drawer. He tossed out a layer of clothing. The false bottom was so neatly fitted that it defied detection, even with the drawer empty. By a secret catch, Van opened it like a hinged door.

The first object he took out was a flat leather kit. The lid snapped open at his pressure, revealing a small but complete array of vials and tubes. Enough of a variety of makeup here to supply any character actor, for any part. This was all he kept in his apartment. When the supply gave out he replenished it from another, more fully stocked source.

Van's well-formed features stared out at him as he adjusted the mirrors. But not for long! For his fingers began to dab stuff from the makeup kit onto his face. A cream dye to change his complexion to a lighter shade. An Oriental preparation, rubbed into his scalp, turned his chestnut hair into sandy color. Tiny bits of hard rubber cartilage in his nostrils changed their shape. A bit of putty on the end of his nose completed the change, making the nose long, pointed.

He was not attempting to make up as any particular person; he was merely creating a face totally different from the face of Richard Curtis Van Loan. There was no time to do more.

In less than five minutes a sharp-nosed face of indeterminate age, topped by sandy hair, stared out at Van from the mirror. Satisfied, he turned away to dress himself in a modest business suit.

He took a battered hat from his closet, then, from the secret compartment of the dressing table took three more objects. The first was a glistening blue-steel Colt .45 automatic, which he shoved into his coat pocket. The second was a black silk domino mask, with elastic attached.

It went carefully up his sleeve, concealed there. The third he had to take from a small plush-lined box. As the box was opened, a scintillating flash of matchless diamonds sparkled in the bright light.

It was a platinum badge, and the diamond studs on it formed a replica, in design, of that black domino mask.

As Van tucked that badge within a vest pocket he ceased to be Richard Curtis Van Loan. It was as if the badge were some magic charm which erased his personality as a society man.

In that moment he flung off all last thoughts of Muriel Havens, of friends, of human feelings and cravings.

He became truly the Phantom. The Phantom, whose only mark of identity was the diamond-studded platinum badge which, throughout the entire world, could bring obedience and respect from any law-enforcement officer.

Yet it was a badge few had seen. Van used it sparingly. Indeed only when dire necessity made its showing necessary.

He straightened, eyes grim, purposeful, in his disguised face. He was ready-prepared to take up the trail to wherever Pat Bentley's dead body might lead him.

Chapter VI
In the Elevator

Short minutes later, Van Loan emerged from a side door of the big apartment house, having descended in another private elevator that let him out that way unseen.

He walked out on the side street, and even his walk was totally unlike that of Richard Curtis Van Loan. It was a shuffling gait which was at the same time rapid. Hurriedly, yet unobtrusively, he moved to the corner, glanced down the Park Avenue block.

He saw two police radio coupes and a detective cruiser. On the sidewalk, surrounded by a crowd which had materialized out of the night, was a little knot of bluecoats and plainclothes men hovering over the corpse. A sudden flash for a Homicide photographer's camera threw them all into relief. The routine investigation was under way.

Avoiding that block, the Phantom walked up the avenue and hailed the first cab that passed.

A five-dollar bill, waved at the taxi man, resulted in a speedy, light-defying ride all the way down to Grand Central.

But as Van alighted from his taxi he saw with frowning surprise that a whole array of police cars were lined before the stone facade of the huge railway terminal. What was more, when he entered the terminal and walked down a ramp into the immense dome-ceilinged concourse, he found himself in the midst of a grim, tumultuous scene.

Crowds, fearful yet curious, were being herded back by perspiring bluecoats. A whole area of the concourse floor, under one gallery, was being roped off by the police. There and in the gallery itself, flash-bulbs were going off at spasmodic, lightning intervals.

Even as Van Loan looked, two pairs of dark-uniformed men hurried across the tiled floor, each pair carrying between them a large wicker basket. Morgue attendants! Evidently coming for two bodies!

This, whatever it was, must be the reason Havens had been about to call him. Something big had happened here. Yet the Phantom did not stop to investigate it now. He must stick to his trail which had begun with the body on the sidewalk-the body he believed to be that of Pat Bentley. After that he could return to whatever was going on here.

He crossed the wide, marble floor, passing train-gates and noting their numbers. Track 41. He was approaching it now.

A group of railway police, some bluecoats and plainclothes men, stood grouped around the gate, all looking confused and worried.

Van Loan approached the gate with the manner of a man who knows where he is going. He hoped he would not have to use his platinum badge to get through.

In a businesslike way he strode directly to the gate, banking only on his knowledge of psychology. His whole air was so completely that of a man who had a definite right to go through that gate, that the group gathered there scarcely gave him a glance.

Walking down the ramp to the platform of Track 41, his eyes peered keenly into the dim, wide tunnel where bells clanged and trains moved in two directions.

The platform was crowded. On the track alongside, with sounds of compressed air still issuing from its brakes, stood the train he sought, its big electric engine humming at the bumper.

The passengers, standing by their baggage, were making loud protests. Railway police and bluecoats who were guarding them were giving weak answers to the protests.

So Havens had carried out his instructions.

Van's keen eyes searched the crowd. All looked like average people —a smattering of business men, a few families, sleepy-eyed, crying children, buxom mothers. And denim-clad men of the train crew and angry-looking conductors.

"Is everybody off the train?" Van asked one of the railway police, his tone officious.

"Yes, sir," the man replied without hesitation, evidently assuming that this sandy-haired stranger had authority. "We have everybody from the train right here."

The Phantom wasn't satisfied. He was not even remotely suspicious of anyone in this crowd. Turning on his heel even as a bluecoat started to move toward him half challengingly, Van slipped aboard the train, hurried through empty Pullmans toward the rear, which he had noted was unguarded, his hand close to the pocket where his .45 nestled.

The last car was not a Pullman, but a coach. It was empty, he saw at a glance through its corridor. He hurried through it hastily, glancing at each seat. Nothing there.

When he had reached the open rear doorway where chains swung to form a gate leading to the train's rear platform, suddenly Van's eyes sharpened. Near the closed-off door of one side of the platform, the side overlooking the tracks, he saw a streaky splatter of red on the glass. Blood!

The Phantom's deductions had been grimly corroborated. This, no doubt, was where Pat Bentley had been shot! Then the pilot had fallen or jumped off the rear of the train.

Van glanced out of the rear, down the darkening tracks. Were the rest of his deductions correct? The train had not been here long. It had been searched, all passengers seen getting off stopped. But there were no police behind this rear, open door!

Yet the tracks behind the car were obviously deserted and —

Again Van's eyes focused narrowly, keenly.

Behind the train, cut through the terminal platform, was an immense steel structure. A freight elevator shaft, open on all sides, running up to the next level.

The elevator in that cage was moving! Slowly it was moving upward-yet it contained no baggage. But Van could glimpse shadowy figures in its open but dim interior. Shadowy figures who seemed to be shrinking there, blending with the gloom.

With swift suspicion firing his muscles, the Phantom dashed from the train, hurled himself toward the ascending elevator. It was already halfway up.

The Colt whipped from his pocket as he ran. His thumb snapped back the safety-catch which guarded its hair-tuned trigger.

"Stop that car!"

His voice cracked out in the crisp command as he raised the gun.

The answer was swift. So swift that, had it not been for his alert intuition, Van would not have ducked so swiftly, leaping behind one of the concrete pillars.

Three livid spurts of red leaped from the darkness of the open-fronted car. Three shattering reports of heavy-calibered automatics crashed through the tunnel. Two of the bullets ricocheted from the post where the Phantom stood, chipping concrete.

The elevator kept rising.

Van waited, even as he heard a commotion at the other end of the platform, where the railway police and bluecoats were whirling toward the sound of the shots.

But the elevator was disappearing into the gloom of another level. The Phantom, savage determination in his eyes, darted from his hiding place as he saw that the occupants of the cage no longer could get a good shot at him.

He saw no access to the floor above immediately at hand. The bottom of the elevator was well over his head. The well of the shaft gaped deep below, with its cable-wheels turning down there.

The Phantom braced his lithe muscles, timed his distance. Then deliberately he leaped into the open shaft, leaped upward, both arms flinging overhead.

His right hand caught supports on the bottom of the ascending elevator. His left hand followed-and he dangled there, momentarily over space, being hoisted up with the car.

Some common sense portion of his brain told him the folly of the risk he was taking. But some stronger feeling spurred him on.

Police were running down the platform, but Van knew they could give him little help now. Clinging desperately to the ascending elevator, he looked upward.

The square of the next floor was looming. It would soon cut off the open front of the elevator. Unless he hurried —

With painful effort Van squirmed his way to the very edge of the shaft's open fronting, fervently hoping that the occupants of the elevator were unaware of their extra passenger. Again he measured distance, judged time.

If he failed to make that landing his body would be crushed like so much pulp!

With his legs doubled up beneath him he reached up with one hand, up past the open fronting, until he had hold of the floor of the elevator. With a grunting heave, he got the other hand around and up, so that he was now clinging to the floor's edge.

The square outline of the next floor was coming down like some grim guillotine. Gathering all his strength then, with one mighty heave, Van chinned himself up past his hands, scrambled onto the elevator floor, was in the cage just as the beams of the oncoming floor closed off the front.

His gun, momentarily pocketed, was out with lightning speed. Even as he got his balance he was training it on four shadowy figures who were shouting in hoarse surprise. Flickering terminal lights from the floor suddenly lighted their faces, under their low, slouch hats.

The smallest of them seemed to be the quickest. He moved with a sort of jerky nimbleness. Flashily dressed, hatless, with patent leather black hair, and an olive-skinned face, he would have been handsome save for the livid zigzag scar on one cheek.

"Watch it, guys!" he snapped in a quick, jerky staccato of authority. "Ape —*your* job!"

A huge, barrel-chested thug, with a flat-nosed face and gash of a mouth, and something simian in the way he swung his arms suddenly charged across the car. One of those arms rose.

A blackjack in the huge hand arced back.

On the balls of his feet, the Phantom sidestepped the big man's unexpected lunge. The blackjack whistled viciously through space-missing his head by scant inches. But he was still unable to bring his gun to bear before the thug fell upon him bodily.

"Okay, Slick! Okay!" Ape's coarse voice yelled. "I got him! Leave him to me!"

The big thug's left arm encircled Van's head in a crushing grip as the elevator came to a stop. A dim floor, filled mostly with baggage and piping, lay beyond its open front. The Phantom struggled fiercely, gasping for breath in the viselike hold of his burly antagonist. With his right hand, the thug was trying desperately to swing the blackjack again.

The flashy, scarred man called Slick was making a gesture with his gun at the other two men whom Van had barely glimpsed in the flickering light. One was tall, with an angular, immobile face. He seemed to move without animation, holding his gun behind an unbuttoned overcoat.

The other man, who was holding a cloth-wrapped bundle, was squat, his head low on wide shoulders, his features crooked, as if each half of his face had lifted or lowered a little.

"Come on, guys!" Slick's staccato snapped. "Gotta scram before the coppers come. Finish that bird, Ape, whoever he is."

As if assuming that Ape could well handle the job, the others started scrambling off the stalled elevator.

Van's head was swimming from the pressure of the big, flat-nosed thug's grip. But inwardly he rallied his own strength, remained cool even though his gun-arm was twisted out of reach.

He spread his feet a little to give him support on the flooring. Then suddenly his whole body, including his gripped head, moved like a springing bow, arcing swiftly with strength and skill.

With a surprised yell the huge, burly thug, heavy though he was, went flying off his feet. The force of the hurtling motion had made him relinquish his terrible head-lock hold.

He sprawled heavily to the floor, dazed surprise on his flat, gash-mouthed face. A clever trick of jiu-jitsu, an art which the Phantom had mastered from the Japanese champion, Soji Kamuri, had come to Van's aid.

With camera-click speed, the Phantom brought his gun around, started for the big thug on the flooring.

Just as quickly he leaped back, ducked behind a protruding steel support of the elevator. Slick and the tall, angular thug had whirled. Their automatics blazed simultaneously, the tall thug firing from the hip.

Van snaked out two shots in return, but he was ducking ricocheting lead and could not properly aim.

Before he could aim, Ape had rolled off the elevator. With the alacrity of desperation, the big man catapulted to his feet to join his companions. All four, with the squat, wide-shouldered one carrying that cloth-wrapped bundle, dashed away in full flight now.

Chapter VII
In Terror's Grip

Quickly the reason for that hasty flight was apparent. Bluecoats and railway police were surging from the top of a stairway, with guns drawn. With the instinct of rats the four thugs were scattering for the dark labyrinths of the pipe-filled rooms beyond.

And only the Phantom, recovering his breath after his brief but hectic encounter with Ape, saw that murderous quartet disappearing. The bluecoats and railway men were merely milling about confusedly.

Bitterly sensing that the thugs had made their getaway, Van moved across the elevator floor. Something caught his eye, stopped him momentarily. From the floor he picked up a torn bit of cardboard.

In the dim light he saw that it was part of a torn railway ticket. On it was the name: Mulford, New York.

It had lain close to the spot where he had hurled the big thug. Had it fallen from Ape's pockets? "Hey, *you!*"

The gruff, challenging shout jerked him up. As he had walked off the elevator, quickly thrusting away the piece of ticket, several police and railway officers suddenly confronted him in an ominous, blocking group, hands on guns.

The four thugs had eluded them and now they glared at this fifth, sharp-nosed man with suspicious hostility.

"Who are you?" a plainclothes detective demanded. "You came in and started giving orders-then we find you mixed up in a gun-fight! Keep your hands still!" he warned, as Van's arms started to move.

The Phantom's eyes hardened, then he relaxed as his decision came to him. He did not offer resistance when the detective strode forward, frisked him hastily, and took away his gun. He drew a breath of relief that the search had been too hasty for the officer to discover the hidden domino mask, the platinum badge and the ticket he had just tucked away.

"My advice to you," Van said, in a cool, level voice, "is to scour the Terminal for four thugs."

Quickly, tersely, he described the four from his brief but retentive glimpses of the quartet. Something in his tone evidently impressed the big detective in charge. He sent bluecoats on the search, told them to get help.

But then his hard eyes swiveled again to the sharp-nosed, mysterious man before him.

"Well, I'm still asking you-who are you? What's your business here? How do we know those guys you described are gunsters? Maybe it's you who're in the wrong!"

"I suggest," Van said in the same level tone, "that you let me see whoever is in full charge down here, at present. I believe I can identify myself properly then."

The detective, eyes narrowed, reluctantly agreed. At his orders, Van was ushered by two of the bluecoats and the detective himself across the floor, through a doorway, down another ramp, up marble stairways.

Quite suddenly, the party emerged onto the gallery surrounding the huge, domed terminal concourse. Van's eyes went with interest around the balcony where he had seen that police activity. But, though police were still there, the commotion had quieted.

Then on the floor below, Van saw the same pair of morgue attendants. They were leaving with the two wicker baskets, heavy now. The bodies were being taken away!

The big, square-faced detective ordered Van taken to the north end of the gallery. Entering a lavishly furnished suite of offices through a frosted glass door, the Phantom realized he was in the executive offices of the Empire and Southwest Railway.

He was brought to a halt in a large anteroom, brightly illumined, modernistically furnished. Two other doors led to inner offices. One was closed. On its wood panel was lettered:

PRIVATE

The other door was open and through it came a hum of tense voices. Van caught a glimpse of several shifting figures, bobbing heads.

Then, at the big detective's call, a familiar figure emerged from that office-and Inspector Thomas Gregg, head of Manhattan's Bureau of Detectives, confronted Richard Van Loan.

Well Van knew this hard-faced detective chief, whose fleshy, placid face belied the grim alertness in his keen eyes. But there was no recognition in Inspector Gregg's eyes now as, listening to the detective's hurried explanation, he narrowed his gaze on the disguised Phantom.

"Well?" he demanded, in the gruff, barking voice that had broken down the reserve of many a hardened criminal. "What have you got to say for yourself? Talk fast! If you're mixed up in this affair it's not going to be so good for you! What were you doing down at that train?"

Van Loan hesitated. All he would have to do would be to let the inspector catch a brief glimpse of his diamond-studded badge, and no more questions would be asked. But that meant openly coming into the case as the Phantom. Coming into a case which already he saw was full of baneful ramifications he had not foreseen. If he were to allow it to become known that he was the Phantom, might that not prevent his having a free hand?

Yet there seemed no other way, if he was to pursue an immediate course of investigation. His platinum badge was his only means of identification, his only proof. And so, reluctantly, he reached into his vest pocket, his fingers closing on the valuable emblem.

Then, with a sudden thrill of gladness, he released the badge-let it drop back unseen.

For at that moment a newcomer came striding hurriedly into the anteroom. A rugged, elderly man with keen, alert eyes. Frank Havens, owner of the *Clarion*!

The inspector, recognizing the influential publisher, gave a respectful greeting. Nodding, Havens's keen gaze darted about the room. His eyes swept Van, passed the Phantom-unrecognizing. Then quickly, Van spoke:

"Say, Mr. Havens, will you tell the inspector that I'm working for you? That you sent me here?"

As Havens's eyes swiveled to the sandy-haired, sharp-nosed man, Van quickly made a strange move. With a gesture that seemed merely nervous habit, he reached up and tugged at the lobe of his left ear.

A gleam of comprehension lighted Havens's eyes. He stepped forward.

"What's the matter, inspector?" he asked crisply. "This man is one of my crime reporters-Elwood Mason." He was quick to invent a name. "I sent him to get facts on this case."

Instantly the inspector's attitude changed. Van's gun was handed back. The Phantom's eyes veiled his satisfaction. Havens, the one man who knew his true identity, could always be depended upon. The ear-lobe tugging, a signal arranged between them, always told Havens what Van's ingenious disguises so often hid.

"Glad to see you, Mr. Havens," the inspector said, and he was. The *Clarion* had always given the police department the breaks. "As for the facts here-Well, I've been trying to get 'em myself. Come along in. You too, Mason."

The inspector ushered them into that inner office. Havens and Van were introduced to the tense gathering whose voices Van had heard from outside.

Some of them, James Strickland for instance, Van recognized on sight. Others he placed by their names.

Strickland, the railway vice-president, was standing behind the long conference table, his florid face a picture of dejection and horror. Next to him stood Charles Jenson, mild-eyed, spectacled secretary of the line.

Four other men completed the group. Men whose names and reputations in the field of science were well-known to Van.

Leland Sprague, wiry, shock-headed surveyor. Donald Vaughan, solidly built but weary-eyed geologist. Paul Talbert, the tall, military-mustached shoring engineer. And finally, quiet-faced, but with dark, frightened eyes, Joseph Ware-the waterways expert.

If Strickland and Jenson looked shaken, these other four seemed to be in an almost paralyzing grip of terror and horror! Van could see it in their haunted eyes, their pale features. Only Talbert seemed to maintain a certain calm; but his hands worked nervously at his sides, giving him away.

James Strickland stepped forward, recognizing Frank Havens.

"Mr. Havens! I've been waiting to hear from you! That order you gave over the phone to hold the passengers of the Buffalo train! We can't hold them much longer or we'll have lawsuits on our hands!"

Havens's eyes flashed a worried glance toward the Phantom. Van spoke quickly. "That tip we had about the train, Mr. Havens, was *bona fide.*" He compounded fact with prevarication smoothly. "There were some gunmen aboard, but they got away. So I guess it's no sense holding the passengers any longer."

"Gunmen?" Strickland blurted. "Damn! Has something else happened on this railway?"

Shaken, the vice-president phoned down to the track, ordering the release of the passengers. He also learned, and told the listening group with him, that the thugs Van had described had vanished without any trace.

"Well," Inspector Gregg clipped. "Let's get back to the case in hand."

He began speaking and, bit by bit, aided by an occasional word from Havens who had been acquainted with the matter through his efficient news organization, Van learned the staggering facts of what had happened in Grand Central Terminal.

Chapter VIII
An Empty Glass

Inspector Gregg told Van of the anonymous phone call from Mulford, New York, prophesying a crime in New York at midnight. Mulford! Van touched his pocket where he had a railway ticket from that place. Facts were beginning to dovetail.

The story of the tragedy in the balcony of the concourse followed quickly, Van learned of the huge electric sign, motivated by a device here in the terminal-but started by Garrison, president of the railway, from St. Louis, over the railway's own wires.

The sign had suddenly gone haywire, and a macabre message from the Tycoon had flashed across its flickering lights. A ghoulish prophecy, hideously carried out when an explosion had occurred, killing Brooks, the sign's maker, and Eldridge, a surveyor.

"Brooks and Eldridge must have gone to the box which worked the sign," the inspector said. "We found bits of a bomb of the 'pineapple' type in the shattered box — a planted bomb which went off there and killed these two men."

An effort had been made, Van learned, to contact the railway president, Garrison, in St. Louis. But he had already left the office where the button had been pressed, had rushed in and out of the place so quickly that few had seen him.

Meanwhile, Death had struck down two scientists who were connected with the Empire and Southwest Railway. Nor had they been the first victims! Two others of the same scientific group-Max Garth, geologist, and David Truesdale, mining engineer-had also been doomed. In as horrible, if different fashion.

And not until then did Van know of the airplane disaster.

Pat Bentley, pilot of the doomed transport, he learned, had radioed his frenzied message that the ship was burning, somewhere over Pennsylvania. Andrew Harvey, president of the airline that owned the burned airplane, could have known nothing of the tragedy up to a short time ago, for he had been down at this terminal. Though on what business, the inspector had not been able to learn.

Pat Bentley! Even as the flyer's name was mentioned, Van saw Havens's eyes go hard; saw grief on the publisher's face.

But Havens did not know, nor did the police even dream that Van himself had found Pat Bentley on Park Avenue; that it was Bentley's corpse that had led the Phantom into this diabolical web of mystery and murder!

During the next minutes the inspector received a call from Headquarters, reporting that a body had been found on Park Avenue. It had not been identified. The inspector dismissed that information as something to be attended to later, with no slightest suspicion that it might be connected with this case.

But Van knew now that it was one of the most devilish affairs he had ever encountered. Out of a maze of violence and intrigue, a mysterious, unknown criminal personality had emerged, had imperially taken the center of stage. The Tycoon!

Van's eyes swiveled to the men in the room, to the quartet of frightened scientists. Knowing that he was backed by Havens's influence and authority, he began to ask crisp questions.

"Have any of you others been warned by this so-called Tycoon?"

The men shifted, exchanging quick glances. Then Joseph Ware gave a weary sigh.

"Yes, I've been warned!" he said hoarsely. "This criminal called me up tonight-said I would die tomorrow! And he means it! After what has happened to the others —"

"The police will give you adequate protection," Van assured, and Inspector Gregg nodded grimly. "But these warnings," Van persisted. "What does this criminal want? It seems he is making some sort of demands —"

Before he had even finished this question, he saw the lips of all four men tighten. Their eyes became veiled, secretive. But, a good psychologist, Van saw that Ware-the man who admitted he had been threatened-was weaker in his resistance than the rest.

He concentrated his probing gaze on Ware.

"With your life at stake, Mr. Ware, don't you think you ought to confide what you know to the police? As the best way of enabling them to safeguard you? For it's clear —" he repeated Ware's own words, " —that this means business!"

"Yes! You're right, Mr. Mason!" the distraught Ware cried.

Sprague started to interrupt, but Ware waved him off with an agitated hand.

"What's the difference? Even Andrew Harvey knew that we all are stockholders in this railway!" He looked at Van, jaw tightening firmly. "The Tycoon has been trying to extort the stock we own. Warning us to turn over the shares, which are negotiable, to him or else die!"

Havens, as well as Van, showed interest at the news that these technicians were stock owners.

"But that can't be the answer-extortion!" Strickland broke in, hoarsely. "It's more that someone is trying to ruin this railway! There's been sabotaging of our lines-looting of trains! And Garth and Truesdale, technicians, who were valuable to the railway, were killed. That further cripples the line and its progress!"

"There was some sort of loot on that airplane, too!" the inspector agreed. "That might be the real reason some way was found to crash it."

Strickland spoke again. "Yes, extortion must just be a blind! Why, the very sabotaging that's been going on has been lowering the value of the stock. The criminal would be a fool to do that-if stock is what he wants."

Talbert laughed harshly. "Maybe not such a fool!" he offered, though he had been tight-lipped until now. "Why, didn't Harvey want to buy out this railway, just to get rid of any competition? I didn't swallow his talk about running it in conjunction with his airlines! Extortion is one way of getting stock. Lowering its value by sabotage is a way to get it for a song!"

Both Strickland and Talbert were vehement in their arguments. But the Phantom sensed that there was something else beneath the surface. What it could be, however, baffled him.

"Just how does this Tycoon demand delivery of the stock?" he asked.

Again the four scientists shifted uneasily. Then Ware, who seemed to have recovered his quiet manner, spoke in a calmer tone.

"I was simply told to be ready to give the stock over. I would receive future instructions, I was told."

"We'll be there if you do!" Inspector Gregg promised firmly.

The Phantom keenly eyed the four scientists. Strange, but he was certain that they were all hiding something-that some dark, secret bond lay between them.

However, he knew he could get no more out of them now. He decided to make the next move in his investigation.

Throughout the quizzing and unsatisfactory answers Van had taken cognizance that the name of Garrison, the railway's president who was in St. Louis, had been frequently mentioned. Where did that important official figure in the maze of mystery?

Eyes thoughtful, Van casually remarked that he'd like to look into Garrison's private office; the room with the closed door on the other side of the anteroom.

The door of that office, which Strickland said had remained unopened since Garrison's departure for St. Louis, proved to be unlocked.

Leaving the inspector talking with the harassed men, Van strode into the railway president's private office. Unobtrusively Frank Havens followed him, closing the big door partially behind him.

"Van!" For a brief moment the publisher dropped the pretense of masquerade, spoke in low tones, emotion gripping him. "What do you make of all this business? And how did you happen to get into it, before I called you?"

The Phantom had switched on lights, which flooded the modernly appointed office. "I'll explain that when we have more time, Frank," he said hurriedly. "Right now I want to get what clues I can together."

After a swift glance about the room, he had moved over to give his attention to a flat-topped desk.

"Pat Bentley was pilot of that plane," Havens reminded. "Maybe you remember him. He used to be my ace news commentator." Grief was in his flat tones.

"Yes, I remember him," Van said, with no word about that corpse on Park Avenue. And then a sudden exclamation of interest broke from his lips.

On one side of Garrison's desk, partially hidden by papers, he had found a drinking glass. It was empty, but moisture-and some peculiar whitish substance-clung to its inner surface.

"If I remember correctly, Frank," the Phantom said, after briefly examining the glass, "all those men in the other room claim that nobody entered this office since Mr. Garrison left for St. Louis the other day. Feel this glass, Frank. Touch it carefully. I don't want to spoil any prints that might be on it."

Havens touched the glass surface cautiously.

"Why it's cold-almost ice-cold!" he exclaimed.

"Colder than it should be in this warm room-unless it recently held cold water," said Van, glancing at the electric water-cooler in the corner.

He smelled the glass, studied the whitish particles clinging to it, then carefully wrapped it in a handkerchief and put it in his side pocket.

"Well," he said, "I guess we've got all we can here. Let's go to your office and tackle this affair from every angle together. Then I'll see if there's anything in what I've found here; if they are clues."

Havens nodded and both men moved to the door, out through the anteroom, and into the other office.

The men there were still talking to Inspector Gregg. Joseph Ware was arranging to have police protection because of the threats he had received.

"I don't see why we should be detained any longer!" Talbert was growling, his mustache bristling. "We've been here most of the night now!"

"We'll be getting along right away," the inspector said gruffly. His beetling eyebrows raised as he saw Havens and 'Mason.' "Well, gentlemen? Any fresh ideas? Looks like straight extortion to me. What do *you* think?"

Havens gestured to Van. A smile flickered across the Phantom's disguised, sharp-nosed face.

"I'm afraid I have little to offer," he said deprecatingly. But his hand was unconsciously touching the pocket where reposed the glass he had confiscated, and that torn railway ticket.

As the inspector was starting to dismiss the rest of the group, Van and Havens left the executive offices. With no suggestion of the tight bond of intimacy between them they walked down the balcony steps, across the great concourse.

"My car is opposite the main entrance," Havens remarked.

Van nodded, and they took the long ramp which led out to the crosstown street which usually teemed with traffic at this hour of the night, or rather morning; however, but few vehicles traversed it.

Across the street, near several parked police cars, stood Havens's coupe. The two men stepped off the curb, walking toward it.

They had taken perhaps five steps when apparently without reason, Van gritted a sharp warning. Grabbing Havens with one powerful hand, he yanked the publisher off his feet.

Havens's first natural thought was that a car he hadn't seen was bearing down. But even as Van rapped: "Down, Frank!" the publisher saw that no car was in sight.

The quiet night was suddenly shattered and rent! A blurred but raucous staccato, as if from some demon invisible typewriter, chattered shrilly.

The staccato of a tommy gun!

Chapter IX
Machine Guns

Van, who had seemed miraculously to divine that sudden menace, had Frank Havens down on the pavement now, with his own lithe motions, and was forcing the publisher to roll toward the curb.

A dancing line of flying bits of lead flew as if magically toward the two men, missing them by scant inches. The rain of slugs lifted them-for all tommy guns have the uncontrollable tendency to fly upwards as they are fired-and the bullets whistled over the heads of Van and Frank Havens.

Even in his predicament Frank Havens saw Van twisting out his own Colt. The automatic roared, spitting livid flame. The Phantom was firing, it seemed, at the empty gloom out in the middle of the street. Havens had not seen the two heads and shoulders that for a moment had appeared out there, and then sunk from view, as Van had seen.

Across the street bluecoats sprang from their prowl-cars, started running with drawn guns. But as suddenly as it had set up its chatter, the tommy gun had ceased its blasting.

As Havens struggled to his feet, Van was already up, had catapulted halfway across the street, gun gripped, eyes narrowed to slits.

Van's strong fingers were scooping at a manhole in the middle of the street. He yanked it partially up, pointed his gun downward, fired two shots into the gloomy well below. Almost with the same motion, he was climbing down into the place himself-to the tunnel close below, on top of one of the city's water mains.

His eyes scanned the gloom. Nothing. Again that sense of frustration, though, even as he searched, careful to keep his body flat against the sides of the tunnel wall. He could see that in one direction the tunnel led toward Grand Central Terminal.

"They got away again!" he said. As he climbed out to rejoin Havens his thoughts were savage; and within his pulses surged a fierce anger, a luxury his cool mind seldom allowed.

It had been a clever, a diabolically clever attack! Only because his alert eyes had seen a suspicious movement of that manhole cover had Van been able to anticipate it.

But from whom had it come?

From those four thugs who had first clashed with him in the freight elevator?

That manhole could easily have been reached through the tunnel from the terminal. But those men had not had a tommy gun-unless it had been wrapped in that cloth-wrapped package the one crooked-faced thug had carried.

Of one thing, however, the Phantom was grimly certain. The brain behind that previous attack on himself was that of the criminal behind this whole intrigue of blood and murder!

The reason for this last attack seemed plain enough. Though no one could have guessed that he was the Phantom, it was known-or reasonably suspected-that he had picked up some clues. Doubtless the criminal had ordered the attack to keep him from making use of them.

Those six railway and technical men had known he had something, must have known from the way he had spoken to the inspector. Van had watched them for some reaction, but seen none. But now he wondered. Right after he and Havens had left, that group had broken up.

Could one of them have been behind the attack?

At least, Van decided, as he climbed to the street, where the dazed Havens was ringed by questioning police, this proved to him that he had discovered vital clues. The glass in his pocket had not been broken; the handkerchief wrapping had protected it.

He made no explanation to the police.

"Mr. Havens," he said hurriedly, "I have an errand-uptown. I'll meet you at your office later. Can you wait for me there?"

But before Havens could answer, could ask questions, the Phantom's lithe figure had slid off into the night.

* * *

Day had broken over the city, and the morning sun was beginning to slant through the high windows of the mid-town *Clarion* Building, in whose depths the pounding rotary presses made a steady vibration.

Seated at his great mahogany desk in his luxurious office, his eyes red-rimmed from sleeplessness, Frank Havens had just turned off the electric lights when the frosted glass door opened discreetly-and Richard Curtis Van Loan strode in, smiling a tight greeting.

Van no longer wore a disguise. Once more he was the impeccable, handsome socialite.

"Morning, Frank," he drawled. "Now we can get down to cases. Sorry if I kept you waiting. Had to make a trip to my laboratory to set things going."

He lighted a cigarette, took a chair near Havens's desk without really relaxing. Though he had been up all night, he showed no signs of fatigue. His eyes were alert, keen.

"Any fresh news, Frank?"

Havens told what he knew. The police had furnished protection for Joseph Ware, the threatened waterways man. And upstate the army was helping search for the wrecked transport plane on which Garth and Truesdale had been passengers.

"They've covered hundreds of miles in a scouring circle from where that plane was when last heard from," Havens said, shaking his head. "They even tried to carry on the search by night, with flares. But they can't find a trace of the wreck."

Van nodded, grimly. Then he reached into his pocket, drew out a large folded aviation map. He arose and laid it down on Havens's desk.

The publisher saw that it was a detailed map which included the states of New Jersey, Pennsylvania, and New York. On it, was a large circle, drawn in ink.

"I suggest, Frank," Van said very quietly, "that you get in touch with all aviation search units, and tell them to move their search to this area that I've marked here in New York!"

Havens's eyes went wide. "But Van!" he protested, checking over the circle. "That's fully a hundred miles from the terrain they've been searching. It's in the Catskill Mountains! What on earth makes you think that a plane flying over Pennsylvania —"

"A hunch," Van said simply, as Havens, despite the fact he was accustomed to these uncanny tips from the Phantom, stared at him amazed. "Of course it may be wrong, but it's worth a try."

Havens did not hesitate. Reaching for a phone, he called Miller Field and the Newark Airport. He repeated Van's suggestions.

When he had completed the calls, he shook his head.

"They can't understand it, Van. Say that would be way off the beacon-But they're desperate enough to try anything."

Van had already dismissed the subject, turned to another. "Any word about Garrison, the man they couldn't contact in St. Louis?"

"No, Van. None that I know of."

Van's eyes half closed. "I'm rather interested in both Garrison and that railway-in which technicians own stock. Suppose you dig up all the data you can on that subject. Perhaps it will tell us some more about these crimes."

Havens smiled, and shrugged. "I've already ordered the men in charge of the *Clarion* morgue to look into the files." He switched on an interoffice phone, spoke briefly. "Hurry up with that data. Send it up to my office as soon as it's ready."

He turned back to the Phantom. "I've also checked up on those scientists, Van. And I learned something odd. Before they came to work for this railway-quite recently-all of them were working for the Government! They were mapping out a Government airport which is to be built in Nevada next year. When they finished that job, they resigned from the Government service and took their present positions."

Van's eyes flickered slightly at this news.

"That *is* peculiar! And now they are stockholders in the railway." He considered a moment, blew out a thoughtful puff of smoke. "Frank, I'd like to get full details on their former work.

The Department of Commerce must have the maps they made of the Nevada field. See if you can get them for me."

"I'll do my best. It will take some time though, I'm afraid."

The publisher broke off as a knock came at the door. Instantly Van Loan relaxed, assumed the languid manner associated with him in his character of wealthy socialite. A man wearing a green eye-shade entered with a great sheaf of papers, clippings, books. He deposited them on Havens's desk and unobtrusively departed.

Both Van and Havens were expert at swiftly gleaning the gist of such data, of reading between the lines. For some time they pored over the mass of printed matter dealing with the Empire and Southwest Railway.

Stories of the line's various operations. Stock quotations. Diagram maps. The lines operated most extensively, of course, in the Southwest.

"It's in the Southwest, too," Havens commented, studying some data, "that most of the sabotage of the railway-looting of trains, even wrecks-has been occurring."

Van nodded. "And you could add, Frank, that the Southwest is the one part of the line that seems best to have withstood the Depression. But from these stock quotations the whole railway was in a slump before any sabotage began. The stocks have been absurdly low. Those technicians certainly cannot consider themselves wealthy in owning their shares!"

He paused, brow furrowed as, turning the clipping, he came to a photograph. A strong, hard face peered out of the picture —a face with bushy brows, black eyes, hard, thin lips, iron-grey hair brushed tightly back.

Beneath was the caption:

Winston B. Garrison

"And here's the elusive president," Van said musingly.

"Yes, I've met him," Havens remarked. "A hard-fisted man, Van. Something of a penny-pincher. He inherited the railway from his father who built it across a wilderness, fighting Indians, going through all the vicissitudes of a pioneer. His son took over, and began expanding the whole line in boom times. Naturally, when the depression came, he had too many tracks-too many trains."

"Yes, that's easily seen. He has many spurs in the Southwest-in several states." The Phantom crushed out his cigarette in an ash-tray. "Frank, everything I've learned so far has told me the criminal behind this mystery is after something big-bigger than we can guess! I've got to find out what it is." Carefully he scooped up the clippings. "I'm going back to my laboratory now. I'm convinced I'm on the right trail-but there's one other thing I want you to do." He hesitated, then said brusquely: "Get all the stuff you have on Pat Bentley!"

"Bentley?" Havens echoed, as a fresh pang of grief plainly stabbed him. "Where does he fit into the picture? It was just his misfortune that he happened to be piloting that transport."

Van's lips drew tight. But still he did not tell Havens yet about that corpse. Though he could trust Havens with any secret, he felt that he should first corroborate all he had deduced. The corpse had not been yet identified. If it had been the police would have informed Havens immediately.

"I'm particularly interested in Bentley's work," Van said. "Get me anything you can on that."

And then, not wanting to draw attention to his keen interest in the hapless pilot: "Don't forget that Department of Commerce map, Frank. Also, on another map, I wish you'd have some one on your staff mark out-and keep marking-the exact locales where the railway is being sabotaged or looted. Keep it going as a sort of running reference."

Having given these instructions, Van once more left the anxious Frank Havens-strode out of the office.

After riding down in the elevator, he emerged on the ground floor lobby as the morning shift were coming to work, some of them glancing at this wealthy young socialite as if surprised to see him up so early.

Suddenly Van drew in a sharp breath.

A slender, dark-eyed girl in a sports dress had entered the foyer. Muriel Havens! Here, doubtless, to see her father.

Another moment and she would have seen Van. But in that moment, changing his very walk, he blended quickly with the throng, avoiding her-and stifling again the quick ache in his heart.

Chapter X
Laboratory Test

On a squalid east side section of the Bronx reared a ramshackle brick loft which no one gave a second glance.

The real estate agent who had formerly had it on his hands had felt that manna had dropped from heaven when an old, stooped-shouldered, grey-haired man, giving his name as Dr. Bendix, had bought the building for a modest sum.

And only Frank Havens knew that Dr. Bendix was–the Phantom! That this was another of the varied roles which Richard Curtis Van Loan lived.

Arriving there quietly and making his way to a back door of the old loft off the street, Van pulled out a ring of keys. Keys which opened a multiple lock that made the house virtually impregnable.

Entering, he walked up one flight of dusty stairs into a large chamber where he had left lights burning. And it was like stepping from some dead past into a modernistic future of scientific marvels. A crime laboratory that rivaled the famous one at the French *Surete,* and that had as many instruments as the Berlin police laboratory, was nested in that deceptive building. Retorts, rows of bottles holding varied chemicals, reposed on the many shelves of the room. Gleaming microscopes and bullet-testing apparatus stood on tables. One entire wall was lined with an immense bookcase, in which were books on crime-detection, on chemistry, physics, and every other conceivable subject. Books written in five languages. From those books the Phantom, poring over pages through many a night, had acquired a knowledge of criminology second only to that of the great Lombroso himself.

Bubbling, hissing chemicals greeted Van with sounds like that of some modern witches' sabbath as, entering, he took off his coat and put on a stained smock. Eagerly he moved to a table where, before his visit to the *Clarion* office, he had left a retort simmering over the flame of a Bunsen burner. Within that retort were the whitish particles he had taken from the drinking glass he had found in Garrison's office. Aside from that powdery white stuff the glass had been a disappointment to Van. It had yielded only smudgy, unidentifiable prints.

Putting on insulated gloves, Van lifted the retort, glanced at it. Tiny, segregated crystals danced in it, having assumed definite shape.

Carefully he poured off the hot liquid chemical and captured the crystals in a small steel strainer. Thence some of them were transferred to a glass slide, placed under a 500-power microscope. The Phantom put his eye to the tube, turned the focusing handles. The crystals became immense patterns; with a clear structure. From the bookcase he drew out a volume on chemistry, flipped its pages. He read:

> "In cold water, will effervesce violently and briefly, throwing off the tartrates and citrates."

He dropped the crystals in a test-tube. Another test-tube he filled with cold, filtered water. Quickly he poured half of it into the first, then just as quickly screwed the mixture tube beneath a large, pyrex-glass retort, turned upside down. Already a bubbling had begun in the test-tube. The water became a boiling froth, rose rapidly. In seconds a wet mist accumulated in the retort above as the effervescence ceased.

Van seized the retort, unscrewed it, turning it right-side up. He poured a fresh chemical into it, and a muggy, bluish liquid appeared.

He gave a sigh of satisfaction. The experiment was finished. He had discovered beyond doubt what those white particles were.

They were a peculiar bromide substance, with a strong morphine and acetylene content. A depressant drug of unusual strength. It was known under the trade name of "Morphomine."

Because of its strong narcotic content it was rarely prescribed by physicians. Indeed, as Van knew, it could be procured only at five specially licensed drug concerns which he found listed in a directory. And in each case the doctor procuring it had to use his regulation slip supplied by the Federal Bureau of Narcotics, registering the traffic of the stuff.

Morphomine! This was the stuff that had been in the glass recently used in Garrison's allegedly unentered office! The tartrates and citrates had been released in gas when the water was mixed with the powdery remnant, but by adding those chemicals he had selected to the few clinging particles Van had recreated the crystals in their original form.

Van picked up a telephone-another phone with a private wire to the *Clarion* office. He told Havens what information he wanted; and in minutes Havens called him back.

"The Narcotic Bureau got it for me," the publisher stated. "Only one of the druggists you mentioned sold any morphomine of recent date. It was requisitioned by a Dr. Carl Ferris, delivered to his private sanitarium-wait, here's the address." He gave a West End Avenue number. "What's this all about, Van?"

The Phantom's eyes gleamed. "Just following up a clue, Frank. You'll hear from me later." Terminating the conversation, he stood considering a moment.

Then, from a secret, small vault hidden in the wall, he drew out a large black ledger.

The Case-Book of Richard Curtis Van Loan!

In those pages were written the full facts of every case the Phantom had ever tackled. Step by step, his progress and deductions were recorded. It was a book replete with the factual stories of bizarre crime and mystery. Detailed reports which not even Frank Havens had read.

Placing it on a desk Van turned to a blank page. With his fountain pen he wrote swiftly, jotting down what facts he knew; especially the facts about Pat Bentley.

Placing the ledger back into its hiding place, the Phantom strode purposefully across the laboratory to a curtained alcove. He swished the curtain aside, entered.

No actor's dressing room could have approached this alcove in the completeness of its makeup equipment.

There were full length mirrors in which one could see himself at every possible angle. There were shelves of jars and tubes containing makeup. There were floodlights, and a special sun-lamp to create artificial daylight. On a long rack hung clothes of every description, of every nationality-from the rags of a derelict to the turban and robe of a sheik.

The Phantom had discarded the role of Mason, Havens's investigator, because the criminals who had attacked him could identify him in that role. So once more, he did a quick and temporary job with his face. Though, as previously, he was not trying to create the replica of any particular man's face. He merely wanted to surely disguise his own features —

It was near noon when a tall, businesslike individual climbed out of a cab on upper West End Avenue —a man of apparent middle-age, with greying hair and sharp, intelligent features.

The Phantom had reached his destination.

Before him reared a granite, modernized house which looked like a private dwelling, but over whose doorway was engraved:

FERRIS SANITARIUM

Van scanned the building. It had a quiet, subdued air. For a moment he hesitated, then deliberately walked up the few steps to the closed front door that resembled any private house entrance and rang the bell.

He heard its muffled ring, then heard clicking, rapid steps.

The door opened. A blond young woman in a nurse's starched, white uniform peered out. Though her face was attractive enough, under the starched cap which topped her mass of wavy blond hair, there was something hostile in it, too. "What is it?" she demanded crisply.

"I want to see Dr. Ferris about one of his patients," Van said with equal crispness.

"Dr. Ferris isn't here. This sanitarium is closed. We are not keeping any patients at this time."

The words came just a little too glibly to suit Van. She started to push the door closed. But Van moved faster.

Firmly, yet unobtrusively, he put his weight to the door, pushed the nurse back with it. And as she reluctantly retreated, he strode into a foyer smelling of disinfectant, and giving onto a corridor. At its far end of which Van glimpsed, through an open door, part of a white room-apparently an operating room.

The nurse had stepped behind an information desk. Her eyes were angry.

"This is a private place," she snapped. "You have no right to force your way in. Who are you?" She was reaching threateningly for a telephone.

Obviously she was not afraid of him. Yet she seemed in a desperate hurry to get rid of him. The peculiar look in her eyes betrayed furtive haste which the Phantom didn't miss.

And then, Van's whole body went suddenly rigid.

From the other end of the corridor came a sharp, unearthly cry! A man's cry-raised in mortal, blood-curdling agony! A scream which resolved itself into one frenzied word.

"You!"

And on that word the scream stopped-gurgled off in a ghastly, sighing gasp.

The nurse had leaped to her feet, her face going starkly white under her makeup, her eyes bulging with fright. As she stood rooted to the spot, and with the echoes of that scream still ringing, Van's lithe body catapulted past her, his hand yanking out his .45. All pretense was dropped now.

His ears had told him the direction of that scream. He dashed to the end of the corridor, where it turned at right angles. The Phantom did not turn with it, but, gun out, dashed straight into the open door of the operating room.

And even though he was on his guard, he was almost taken completely unaware. The room had seemed empty, and Van had not been prepared for the appearance of the tall figure, with a handkerchief drawn over the face, that suddenly darted out the opposite door.

Two reverberating reports crashed out in swift succession, from the gun in the disappearing man's hand. The Phantom ducked, even as he whirled to glimpse the flash of pistol shots. He heard the slugs whistle over his head; heard the splintering of glass as an instrument case flew to bits.

Van's own gun blazed the moment before the man was out the door, slamming it behind him. Van realized that the glimpse he had had of the fellow had been too brief for him even to take note of the attacker's clothes. And the handkerchief had completely hidden his features.

But Van Loan had seen something else in that brief moment. He saw it as he leaped across the room toward the slammed door. Something bulky and limp in the center of the floor.

Seizing the door and shielding his body by its frame, he opened it. The empty turn of the corridor, with closed doors opposite him, alone met his view. Not a sign of anyone there.

For just a moment he hesitated, deliberating pursuit which he sensed would be futile. Then he turned from the door, crossed the operating room to the thing he had seen on the floor.

Spreadeagled there lay a tall man. His overcoat had been thrown back, and protruding from his chest was the metal hilt of a long bone-handled knife, such as might have come from the sanitarium kitchen. It had been driven into the victim's heart. Blood, a ghastly stain of it, surrounded the knife, and more blood lay in a crimson pool on the floor.

That the man was dead was at once apparent. His eyes were glazed; his face was frozen in a distorted grimace.

Van's own eyes bulged as instant recognition of the man came to him. Joseph Ware, waterways expert of the Empire and Southwest Railway! The man who had asked the police department to protect his life from the Tycoon!

Ware, stabbed to death in this private sanitarium!

Suddenly Van stooped over the corpse. A bit of paper, crumpled in the dead man's outstretched right hand, had caught his eye.

He pried it loose, glanced at it. It was a check, dated this day. It was made out to Joseph Ware for the sum of twenty-five thousand dollars. But what made Van's eyes widen with slow amazement, even in this tense moment, was the signature.

The check was signed by *Max Garth.*

Max Garth, the geologist! One of the passengers on that ill-fated airplane transport. And here was a check, dated this day, made out to a man who could never cash it now.

A sudden hoarse exclamation made the Phantom whirl, gun whipping up.

In the doorway stood a tall, white-coated man. His eyes were two dark pools of horror and amazement as they swiveled from the knifed corpse to Van.

"God!" he gasped. "What —" He stared at Van with suspicious fear.

Van spoke crisply. "Dr. Ferris, I believe?" It was more a statement than a question.

The tall man nodded dazedly. "Yes! But who are you? Who is that dead man?"

But before Van could reply, a fresh sound came to his alert ears.

Muffled, yet distinct, rose a woman's voice-the voice of the nurse. It came from somewhere beyond the second closed door of the operating room.

"No, I tell you, you must stay in bed! You can't get up!"

Chapter XI
Missing Man

Paying no attention to the dazed, horrified doctor, once more Van yanked open the door. The corridor was still empty. The voice must have come from beyond the door across the little hall.

He leaped to open it, plunging into a small white bedroom.

In the middle of the floor, the blond nurse was trying to force a struggling man back onto a cot. Even as Van entered, the man ceased his struggles and slumped onto the bed. He lay there unmoving, as if only half conscious, though he was fully clothed.

The nurse whirled, frightened, to face Van whose eyes roved from the man on the bed to a table nearby, where he saw a bottle of whitish powder. Morphomine!

"He-he's too sick to get up!" the nurse stammered. "Oh, what am I going to do with him! He insists he's going out-has business. He even got into his clothes during the few minutes I left him!"

Van did not answer her jittering.

"Call the police!" he rapped at her. "And don't leave these premises!"

She stared at him, confused. Then Dr. Ferris, in the doorway, broke in hoarsely:

"Yes, Miss Keenan. Call the police at once!" As she ran out, he glowered at Van. "I must ask you to come out of this room, whoever you are!" he said indignantly. "This patient has a bad heart. Any excitement —"

"If he has a bad heart." Van said levelly, "you, Dr. Ferris, will find yourself arrested for malpractice-for giving him morphomine, which no man with a bad heart could safely take!"

A hoarse, croaking cry suddenly came from the cot. The man in the bed was sitting bolt upright, staring at Van.

His face was worn, pallid. His eyes held a burning, bright-pupiled glare. Now and then his whole body —a firmly knit, well-built body, seemed to tremble as if with ague.

No mistaking the identity of that man. Van had recognized him immediately, from a photograph he had seen. He had identified the hard, dominant features, the strong chin which now so incongruously was quivering with weakness.

"What's happened?" croaked the man. "What's going on here?"

"A great deal is going on here —*Mr. Garrison,*" Van answered levelly.

And Winston B. Garrison, president of the Empire and Southwest Railway, sagged back on the pillow, eyes fearful.

"You know me?" he croaked. "Who are you!"

Van did not quibble. He had already decided on his next move. The time had come.

"I am known," he said crisply, "as the Phantom Detective."

"The Phantom?" echoed Garrison hoarsely, while Dr. Ferris, too, stared at the disguised Nemesis of crime. Both seemed amazed to find the famous detective so prosaic-looking.

"Yes," Van said shortly. He turned to the doctor. "I should like to speak to Mr. Garrison privately-before the police come."

The doctor's dark eyes showed hostility, but he went out, closing the door.

"Mr. Garrison," Van clipped to the patient, "I appreciate that you're ill, but the police will be asking you some questions. I thought you might rather talk to me-first. I might be of help to you." As Garrison stared at him wordlessly he said: "Joseph Ware has just been murdered in the operating room. His murderer either escaped or is someone here. The police will certainly notice that your door here is opposite the door of the operating room-and that the nurse discovered you out of your bed!"

Garrison's jaw dropped; his eyes continued to stare in horrified alarm.

"I'm sorry to have to speak so bluntly, but you're in a tight spot," the Phantom pursued grimly. "Especially since you were supposed to be in St. Louis! That alibi is completely shattered! I happen to know you were in Grand Central Terminal last night, where two men were murdered, though none of your associates saw you."

Garrison was straining forward from the bed now, the muscles in his neck bulging like heavy cord.

"Wait," he cried hoarsely. "If you think I had anything to do with these murders, I can explain all that! I'm a sick man. Bad business has wrecked my nerves! But I couldn't let my associates know it. That would have ruined what morale they have left. I sent my secretary to St. Louis. He went into the office there wearing my upturned coat, and pressed the button to motivate the electric sign. I cleared up some papers at my own New York office, then came here, where I've engaged the entire sanitarium-my own nurse, and Dr. Ferris. You can see from my condition —" He paused, gasping, his eyes a plea.

But Van was not forgetting that vigorous struggle with the nurse.

"Tell me, Mr. Garrison, how come that group of scientists acquired shares of stock in your railroad?"

Garrison leaned back on the pillows. "I'll be frank with you, Phantom. This railway has been my life —I promised my father on his death-bed I would always keep it going. But the depression hit the line hard, and it didn't recover. Still I held onto it-didn't want to sell out. My last cent of capital went into it, but it was like pouring water into a sieve.

"Then Garth and the others came to me with a proposition. They offered me plans to modernize the railway, to put new life into it with modern inventions, as streamlined trains. They knew I had no money to hire them-so they demanded shares of stock for their work.

"What did I have to lose?" He gave a harsh laugh, and for a moment Van saw the hard-fisted, penny-pinching business man Havens had described. "The stock was worth little. If their modernization saves the railway it will be their gain. Otherwise nothing is lost. A fair bargain, as you can see."

"Yes," Van nodded, his glance keen. "That is, if on second thought you didn't regret giving them the stock."

"I hardly care any more," Garrison sighed. "For now, with this sabotage and murder, my railway faces ruin! Whatever work they are doing is being undone by enemies! Someone is trying to ruin me-that is certain."

"Have you any particular person in mind?"

"No. Perhaps a rival company, though I can't think of any." Garrison's eyes narrowed, and he seemed less ill. "Of course, Andrew Harvey's been after me to sell out to him for a long time, but —"

He broke off, as the wail of sirens, the squeal of brakes, sounded outside.

Van hastened to the door.

The police were in the place the next instant-detectives from Homicide coming close on the heels of the precinct bluecoats who had responded to the nurse's call.

And this time Van flashed into view the scintillating diamond-studded badge which was his identity.

The Phantom had come into the open!

Inspector Gregg, among the first to arrive, studied the Phantom, whom he had seen in other disguises, or masked.

"So you're working with us, Phantom," he said gruffly, and as always, it was hard to tell whether he was grateful or whether he resented the idea because of official pride. "This whole business is getting under my skin, I don't mind saying. Ware had two precinct detectives with him. What happened? He gets a phone call-and gives them both the slip. They couldn't trace the call, either. And now —"

He pointed to the corpse, the silent chief actor in a drama of flash-bulbs and fingerprinting activity. The quiet sanitarium was a bedlam now inside and out. For reporters from various papers were already showing up, waving press cards and demanding entrance.

Gregg questioned Garrison, the blond nurse and the doctor. All were tight-lipped, but denied any part in the tragedy. The nurse said she had seen no stranger on the premises outside of the

Phantom. She gave her name as Shirley Keenan, and said Garrison had engaged her to work in both night and day shifts.

Garrison said nothing about his faking the trip to St. Louis. Nor did Van mention it. For Gregg was beginning to look at the railway president suspiciously, and Van wanted to withhold that vital bit of evidence until he could satisfy his own mind.

The phone in the office rang as Gregg and the Phantom stood in the corridor. The inspector was called to the instrument.

"Hello-Yes, Mr. Havens," he said with quick respect, and Van's ears pricked up. "Yes, it's true-another murder. And we've found Garrison here! Glad you decided to send the Phantom on the case. He's here now." He nodded to Van. "Mr. Havens wants to speak to you."

Van took the phone, spoke crisply, impersonally, "Hello, Mr. Havens."

"Phantom!" Realizing that Van wasn't alone, Havens used the sobriquet. "I have urgent news for you! They've found the wreck of the transport plane!"

A gleam leaped to Van's eyes. "Yes? Where?"

"In the very area you suggested they search-up in the Catskills, two miles north of Mulford! Two army flyers spotted it, and though it crashed on a sort of plateau, they didn't chance a landing. They report no sign of life. Andrew Harvey, at Newark, is trying to arrange search parties to go up there from Mulford."

Van spoke with quick, sharp decision.

"No-we don't want any bungling there! Have those search parties called off, Mr. Havens. Let the authorities wait until they hear from me. I want to see that scene firsthand!"

Vital clues at that wreck might be obliterated if there was a public search of any sort-obliterated accidentally, or by design.

With Havens's brief, though anxious assent, Van hung up the phone. He did not delay a moment. Even as the stocky medical examiner came striding into the sanitarium with his bag the Phantom dashed out, eyes grim with the knowledge that the biggest break of this baffling case had come!

Chapter XII
Gun Girl

A dull afternoon sun was slanting in the western sky. In its greyish light, the lonely Catskill mountain top looked very desolate and funereal, with all its timber.

Death lay on this mountain.

On a grassy plateau of ground was one charred, ugly swath. Metal, twisted and bent and fire-blackened, lay strewn about it. Two immense Douglas engines, with propellers grotesquely twisted, lay at absurd angles; reduced to so much twisted junk.

And amid this wreckage, which was their only grave, lay the gruesome bodies.

All were burned, charred, and blackened, and in some cases featureless. Skeleton bones showed in some, and even these bones were fire-blackened. Eyes, like baked marbles, stared sightless but as if to call the heavens to their hideous plight.

But among the dead, one living being moved on that mountain top; one man who had used every facility to rush to this scene.

A cab had sped the Phantom to Mitchell Field. Thence he had been flown to the town of Mulford, where there was a small airport. There he had hired a small, serviceable Ford coupe, driven it up the steep mountain road, and cached it just below the plateau.

Now, face stern, he moved among the dead. He was counting those dead. There were twelve of those charred bodies. And aboard that plane had been fifteen persons, including its stewardess and two pilots.

One of the missing, of course, was Pat Bentley, whose corpse still lay officially unidentified in New York. But what of the other two?

Had their bodies perhaps been completely consumed in the holocaust?

Suddenly the Phantom paused in his grim search among the scattered corpses.

A glimmer had caught his eye. It came from the burned, almost skeleton hand of one charred corpse. A ring, platinum.

Gingerly he removed it from the burned hand, lifted it in the greyish afternoon light.

On the inside of the band fine, engraved script met his eye. A name.

David Truesdale!

The famous mining and ventilating engineer, working on the railway staff, who had been on this plane.

Then Van saw something else a little distance from the corpse. A smoke-blackened briefcase, open. He scooped it up, saw that it was made of fireproof material. At first examination it seemed quite empty. But then the Phantom, delving into it, drew out a small, jagged bit of hard, ore-like substance.

He looked at it curiously, then shoved it into an inner pocket; dropping the briefcase for the time being.

He continued his examination of the dead. Brass buttons identified the co-pilot's corpse. Doubtless others would be identifiable. But he could not identify any of them definitely as the stewardess, or as Max Garth. Garth, whose check for twenty-five thousand dollars, dated today, he had found on the murdered Joseph Ware.

Next Van came across some half-melted, broken boxes of metal. Strong boxes. Empty! But on one of them he found an aluminum tag that read:

1500 shares, Empire and Southwest.

Stock! Stock, which Ware had claimed was the Tycoon's extortion demand, had been on this plane!

Van straightened. He gave his mind to the most baffling part of this enigma now. How had this plane, which Bentley, ace flyer, had reported as being over Pennsylvania, crashed here in New York, a hundred miles off the radio beam?

Havens had been astonished that Van deduced it *had* crashed somewhere in this vicinity. But the Phantom had reached that conclusion from two dovetailing clues. The railway ticket he had found on one of the thugs, and the inspector's mention of the anonymous phone call he had received from Mulford.

He had deduced that Bentley, escaping from the plane, had somehow reached Mulford. From there, after calling the police, he had taken that train to Manhattan. Thugs had followed him, killed him. With that as a premise it had been plain enough to Van that the big airplane must have fallen somewhere near Mulford.

But how —

He gave his attention to the plateau then. One edge was fringed with trees. Through them Van could see that the mountain dropped rockily, in a sheer, precipitous cliff.

On the other side the slope was more gradual. The plateau was small, yet —

Van walked over the stubbled ground, pursuing a will-o'-the-wisp thought. And suddenly that thought materialized. He had found twin swathes through the stubble. Two long, even tracks.

His eyes went to slits. The discovery, strangely, brought a surge of fierce anger leaping through his veins.

"The devils!" he gritted.

It was only then that he saw the shack.

Perhaps he would have seen it before except that he had not been looking for any such thing. Besides, the trees screened it well. He strode hurriedly through those trees, gun in hand.

The shack was small but stoutly built, of heavy timber. It had small, dust-grimed windows. The rear of it was backed against the very edge of the steep, precipitous cliff, the top of which was grassy.

The house looked deserted. Van's eyes scanned the grass to either side. He saw two huge metal drums among nearby trees. Gasoline drums!

He did not stop to examine them now, but moved to the shack, tried the door. Locked. He studied the lock as from his pocket he drew a pliable bit of specially tempered steel wire-equipment he seldom failed to carry.

Deftly the Phantom twisted the steel bit into the lock, letting it assume the shape of the notches. It took him less than three minutes to pick that lock.

He swung the heavy oak door of the shack outwards with one hand, covering the dim interior with the gun in his other hand.

But no one was inside. There was not even any furniture. Stepping in, the Phantom's keen eyes roved about the interior. A glint in one corner of the room attracted his glance. Moving toward it he looked down at a tangled mass of wires, broken coils, and large, jutting bits of broken glass tubes, still screwed into sockets. His glance went upward. He saw a hole in the roof, wire coming through it, dangling loose and twisted.

As he moved about, absorbing this evidence, Van's foot kicked something, sent it skittering across the floor. Quickly his eye followed it, and in another moment he picked up a flat small bit of hard rubber. One edge was arced smooth; the others formed jagged sides of a triangle, giving the effect of a flat cut of pie. Parallel grooves ran through the piece.

He looked about but saw nothing else. He pocketed the rubber piece. His eyes were gleaming with grim comprehension. He was ready to turn this place over to the authorities now.

He strode out of the shack; out once more upon the lonely, desolate plateau with its strewn, charred dead and —

A sudden snarled shout froze his blood!

Even as he stiffened in the greying afternoon light he saw diving figures materializing on that plateau.

Over the slope, and from trees they appeared-slouch-hatted, charging men, guns glinting in their hands. One and all, they were charging toward Van!

And even as they plunged forward Van recognized familiar faces. The olive, white-scarred face of the man he had not long ago heard called "Slick," a flashy, sport-coated, nimble figure who was giving jerky commands. The square, crooked face of the squat, wide-shouldered man-and that of the tall, angular thug. The three who had mixed it with the Phantom in that railway terminal conflict.

Van ducked back in a defensive crouch. The sight of a mob of thugs charging upon him roused him to reckless rage. His Colt, at his hip, jerked in his hand. Two quick, blind shots crashed on the mountain top, as his automatic blazed.

A ratty-looking gunman in the charging group screamed, clawing at a shoulder while blood spurted out between his fingers. Others momentarily fell back. The Phantom darted for the nearest tree-trunk, as Slick's voice ripped:

"Let him have it, boys!"

Guns blazed. A whole fusillade of bullets smashed through the trees, chipping bark. Van's lithe body slid all the way behind a tree trunk. He must find some means of retreat or they'd have him! His Colt snaked out, firing again-and again the gunmen felt the grim wrath of the Phantom, as another fell, wounded.

A crunch of underbrush behind him made Van whirl. Just in time to glimpse a huge, burly figure leaping upon him with a snarled cry. The flat-nosed, gash-mouthed thug called Ape!

In his loping, simian-like attack, the big mobster was upon the Phantom before the latter could bring his gun to bear. Van went down under the sheer weight of the man. Down, struggling, to the grassy turf, with Ape's murderous face above him.

With a gritted oath, Van tried to roll the big man off. But instantly the others were rushing to the scene. More of them fell upon the prone Phantom. Blows from revolver butts banged against his head and body. Kicks jarred his ribs, brought agonizing gasps from his lungs.

Half stunned, he felt Ape's weight lifting as the big man rose. He himself was yanked to his feet, to find himself ringed by some dozen thugs, with the two he had wounded groaning on the ground beyond.

Rough hands frisked him. His Colt was already gone. But helpless though he was, the Phantom, by a secret legerdemain which he had never revealed to anyone, managed to keep other articles undiscovered. A diamond-studded badge, a black domino mask, as well as the bit of hard rubber he had found, were concealed on his person.

The quiet, crooked-faced gangster was leveling a gun at him.

"Let me give him a bellyful right now, Slick," he begged with evil eagerness, finger tightening on the trigger.

"Hold it, Maxie, hold it!"

The jerky command came from Slick who stepped forward authoritatively, a nervous hand toying with his gun. He was hatless, as usual, his plastered-down hair making a familiar black, shiny knob of his head. He came forward to the Phantom, dark eyes flashing. And Van was thankful that his disguise could stand the late afternoon dimness.

"Yes." A quick nod from the appraising Slick. "This is him all right. Same feller we mixed it with in Grand Central. I got a good gander at him if the rest of you didn't. Probably a private 'tec somebody's hired to horn in, but anyway the boss'll be wantin' to know about it, wantin' to have a little talk with this guy. I'm just figuring what we can do with —"

"You can stop figuring right now, Slick!"

The sudden new voice made Van start as violently as it did the others. It was a woman's voice!

Through the crowd came a slender, shapely girl. She was hatless, and in the dimming light her hair was a wavy mass of red. She was heavily rouged, too. She carried a small revolver, and her grip on it was one of confidence and experience.

Van stared at her as she came to Slick's side. Who was she? What did her words mean? A reprieve?

"Kitty!" Slick's voice was an annoyed rasp. "What the hell did you come up here for? This ain't no place for a moll right now!"

"No?"

Van saw how hard her face was; saw the peculiar icy glint in her eyes. He had seen the type before; the type of gun moll who could be more vicious, more cold blooded, than men who followed the same calling.

"No?" she repeated, her eyes flashing. "Well, I didn't come up here just to look at your dirty mug!" She spoke with heat, and the look she gave Slick told Van more than her words did. "Not that I ever get a chance to see you lately. I don't, if you can steer clear of me!"

"Aw, lay off, Kitty!" Slick complained. "We got business here. This bird's somebody the boss'll be wantin' to see. He's been follerin' us, tryin' to mess things up. We got to do something with him —"

Her eyes flashed to Van, hate flaming in them. Then she gave a shrill laugh.

"You're telling *me* he's been messing things up! That's rich. Listen, Slick —"

She pulled the gang lieutenant to one side, and for moments spoke swiftly, eagerly. Van saw the deep frown that settled on Slick's face, saw the hate that filled the gangster's eyes as they flashed to the Phantom. But there was exultation in those eyes as Slick turned from Kitty and faced the gang.

"Fellers," he announced, with staccato triumph, "this ain't no cheap mug we've grabbed! He ain't no snoopin' private 'tec. Boys, *we've got the Phantom!*"

A growl of animal-like fury and vengeance rose from every man there, as Van's heart went cold. So they knew! This girl had told Slick who he was, but how in heaven's name had she known? Only those in the sanitarium had seen him identify himself as the Phantom, in this particular guise. Had the tip-off come from someone *there?* Who could have given this girl the information?

"The Phantom! So that's what he looks like!" It was the tall, angular thug who held his gun under his overcoat as he had in the terminal elevator who thus expressed his disappointment. "Not so hot, if you ask me."

"Luke's right," put in the crooked-faced Maxie. "He's just a mug!"

Van hid his one surge of relief. At least they didn't suspect he was disguised. They wouldn't remove that disguise and reveal his true identity.

"The Phantom!" Slick danced up close before him. "Thought you'd pull a fast one, didn't you? Lucky we got here when we did-and that you were sap enough to come alone."

Van was silent. It was true that he had not expected the arrival of the thugs; not so soon anyway. Certainly not the sudden appearance of the red-headed girl with her startling information. Yet he still felt that had he not come alone to view the evidence he wouldn't have learned all that he had. Not that it would do much good now, it was beginning to look like.

He could see his death warrant in every face around him. Yet he remained cool, his mind working, and he was fighting to recover the strength that had been beaten from his body.

"Well, you're finished now, Phantom, see?" Slick announced, more triumphantly. "You won't be sendin' any more boys up the river!" His dark eyes flashed. "The question is now, just how we're gonna give it to you-give it right!"

The girl came forward quickly, grabbing Slick by the arm.

"Wait, Slick!" she commanded. "Listen to what I've got to tell you before you gun him!" Her voice was shrill. "I've got new orders-from the Tycoon! I just had time to bring them. Have to get back right away."

"Thought you had another job scheduled." Slick had drawn her swiftly aside and was speaking to her in a low voice, one that did not reach to the men who were guarding the Phantom. But Van's keen ears caught the gang lieutenant's words.

"That date's for tomorrow, at dawn," the girl answered. Her voice warned. "Gee, Slick, it's good to see you. Even like this. If it wasn't for the way I feel about you, I wouldn't be doing all this."

"Cut it, cut it! What's the Tycoon want?"

To reply, she lowered her voice so greatly that Van could catch but few snatches of what she said.

" —like the others-And then stick these there —" From a handbag she drew out some shiny brass buttons, handed them over with some other articles.

Van saw Slick's olive face pale a little. "Say, I don't like that. Why can't we just plug —"

"I'm telling you what the Tycoon ordered." Her voice was hard. "You think I like it any more than you do? But we've done worse for the Tycoon. What's one thing more?"

Slick looked at her hard features, her cold eyes. "Cripes, Kitty, for a dame you sure got nerves like ice."

His own face hardened, the scar showing livid, evil, as he turned from her. "Okay, boys!"

He jerked out orders.

Chapter XIII
Flaming Death

Cold Apprehension Tightening about his heart, the Phantom still could offer no resistance as once more rough hands seized him. Rope was now produced. While the hard-eyed girl looked on, Van was bound hand and foot, the cords digging into his flesh.

Helpless, he was lifted bodily, carried to the shack. They tossed him in as if he were a heavy sack of meal. He crashed to the floor bruised. The door closed on him, was locked from the outside.

Even as that door closed, though, Van was already trying to struggle against the bonds that held him, using all his skill and strength.

Outside he heard the gang moving about busily. He heard Slick's voice.

"Two of you'll stay here to attend to them brass buttons and stick him with the other stiffs. The rest will scram. Okay, Ape. Let her fly."

There was a grunting sound of effort, apparently from Ape. Then a swish of liquid. A pungent, sweetish odor assailed Van's nostrils.

His blood went cold. Gasoline! From one of those drums he had seen! They were saturating the wooden shack with it. Full comprehension came.

He was going to be burned alive, converted into a charred corpse like those many others! And only too clearly now did he see the criminal's clever, devilish purport.

Those brass buttons would be planted on his corpse. So would the other stuff the girl had brought. Van had no doubt they were effects taken from Bentley! And his corpse would be found and identified as Bentley's.

The criminal was covering his tracks. If the police should learn that Bentley had actually been murdered in New York, the investigation of this whole disaster would be carried to a feverish pitch. If "Bentley" were found here, the crash might still seem an unfortunate accident. The investigation would doubtless die out, especially without the Phantom to carry it on.

Van cursed himself for not having told Havens about Bentley's body. True, if anything happened to him Havens would eventually find his case-book and learn the truth, but by then it would be too late. The criminal would have had further time to cover his tracks.

This thought spurred Van to a desperate frenzy. With all his skill and strength he struggled against the ropes that bound him, battling with every last ounce of power in his body for a way out of his predicament.

The gas fumes choked him. Some of the stuff was already dripping through the small window.

In spite of all his efforts his bonds were as tight as ever. Groaning he managed to roll partially across the floor. By force of will as much as strength, somehow he managed to reach the corner where that broken tangle of wires still lay. Promptly he rolled on his back, working his bound wrists to the broken, jagged glass tube screwed rigidly in a socket near the floor.

"Go on, Slick." That was the gun moll's voice. "Get it over. We don't want to hang around here."

Fiercely, the Phantom's wrist sawed at the broken glass. Shards cut his flesh —

Then — a snap. The cords suddenly parted; his hands jerked loose. In the space of a breath he extricated his feet. Free!

But even as he leaped to his feet there came a hissing roar. The window on the front of the shack became a square of blinding, livid flame.

"Now burn, Phantom!" Slick's high-pitched voice taunted.

Van was lurching toward the door. But, as instantly as he recoiled from it, the wood walls seemed to turn into transparent flaming paper.

The heat seared his flesh, sent makeup rolling down his face, drove him back. The front of the shack was a solid sheet of flame. Black, billowing smoke eddied in, filling his eyes and his lungs at the moment he heard the mobsters breaking up, heard the woman's receding voice.

No possible escape on the front side of the shack. And the windows were all too small for him to get through. Blindly Van stumbled to the opposite wall; the wall that overlooked the steep cliff. His body lurched against it, trying to split the wood. Flame-tongues, yellow gasoline flame, reached for him like fingers of incandescent death.

The rear wall shivered at the impact of Van's hurled body, a large loose board rattling a trifle. Van kicked at it, flung his body at it again and again, ignoring the bruising pain.

And the board split, falling outward. A gaping space, shadowy in the dusk, was revealed-the drop of the cliff. And at the instant that board splintered the flames literally came cascading across the shack interior with a surging roar.

Desperately the Phantom squirmed through the aperture which had helped the flames with its draft. To hesitate for even a split instant now would mean to be instantly engulfed in the roasting fire.

He dropped, his hands clutching the very edge of the cliff. Pendulant, he swung there between flames that seared his knuckles and a drop to sheer, jagged rocks below.

Clinging with one hand, with the other Van started to work his way along the cliff's edge. The shack was a roaring bonfire now, with smoke swirling like a black pall. Suddenly the shack began to topple toward the cliff, threatening to crash down on the Phantom's hanging body.

He doubled his efforts, working his way hand over hand along the cliff, with the heat of the flames scorching him.

Then, even as half the shack tumbled crazily off into space, dropping in a flaming mass, Van was out of the way of it. With his almost exhausted strength he was chinning up a free portion of the cliff edge.

His body rolled onto the plateau, livid in the night from the flames of the half of shack still burning. And the first thing Van did was to reach into his hidden pocket for his black silk domino mask and snap it on over his face, on which the makeup had melted and run.

Two slouch-hatted figures whirled towards him even as he got that mask on.

The two of the mob who had been left to finish this job!

Both cried out in incredulous alarm, as they saw this domino-masked man whom they still could recognize in the flickering glow of the fire as the victim they had thought doomed.

One, a man with a pallid, expressionless face, leaped forward with a snarled curse, whipping up his gun. His companion, tall, with a flat-cheeked face that looked hatchet-like, was slower, because his hands were full. But he dropped the objects he held; reached for his own gun.

A wrench-and Van had the weapon, pushing its owner aside. The second thug leaped, his own gun only half-drawn, grabbing for the Phantom's revolver.

The unexpected bodily attack sent Van hurling backward to the very edge of the cliff. And then the Phantom acted out of sheer desperation.

With a lurch, he swung his attacker full about. His fist doubled into a ball that had iron power, crashed out in a short, but powerful jab.

It crunched against flesh and bone. With a stunned gasp, the hatchet-faced man staggered backward. And before he could stop himself, his swaying body pulled him over the edge of the cliff.

Screaming, the thug hurtled down through space. A ghastly thud below proclaimed his doom on the jagged rocks there.

Breathless, Van was already swinging about to bring his gun to bear on the remaining gunman.

But the latter, unarmed, had had enough! He was already streaking through the trees, down the slope side of the plateau. He had lost himself before Van could even start pursuit.

Savagely panting, his body aching with bruises and burns, the Phantom nevertheless prodded himself to action. That one live gangster now escaping might bring the others back when he reported that the criminals' Nemesis had broken free, had killed the hatchet-faced thug.

Suddenly the Phantom stooped to the ground, illumined by the burning shack. Those objects the hatchet-man had dropped! Quickly he retrieved them. The brass buttons —a watch.

Pat Bentley's watch.

Just as he was about to make his way off the gruesome plateau, a throbbing roar overhead jerked his eyes up. A large Boeing plane swooped low in the sky, wings shimmering. The eagle and star of the United States Army showed on its wings and fuselage.

Army flyers had been attracted by the fire; a fire where the wreck had previously been discovered.

Relieved, Van ran out in the ebbing light of the flames, even as the plane circled low. He waved with both arms, caught an answering wave from the open cockpit. With his thorough knowledge of flying, (he himself had done plenty of it) Van signified that there was room on the plateau for a landing.

The army plane negotiated that landing with ease, by firelight and moonlight. Moaning, it glided in and the Phantom rushed up in his domino-mask, pulling out his platinum, diamond-studded badge —

* * *

Little over an hour later, a tense group of men were gathered in the brightly lighted administrative office at Newark Airport. Andrew Harvey, grizzled airline chief, stood in grim, questioning silence next to the four radio men who had been on duty the night of the big disaster.

At a table Frank Havens, his rugged face tense, was opening a large suitcase, exploring through it.

And before them all, dominating the scene, stood the Phantom in his domino-mask, his eyes gleaming keenly through the holes of the black silk.

The army plane had flown him here, after first circling in an effort to locate the escaped gang. Van had regretted losing track of the mob, yet he was clinging to a conviction he had formed during that macabre experience; a hunch he felt would later put him back on the trail not only of the gang but, what was more important, would lead him to the devilish unknown who was their leader.

The man who called himself the Tycoon!

On his arrival here Van had phoned Havens, asked tense questions to which he had received an assent.

And now —

"This must be it!"

Havens broke the silence, and from the suitcase he pulled out a phonograph record. Van took it silently. The Phantom pulled from his own pocket the bit of hard rubber surface he had found on the shack floor.

Fortunately the heat of the fire had not melted it.

The Phantom compared it with the record Havens gave him. He nodded with quick satisfaction.

There was no doubt in his mind now.

His eyes swiveled to the radio men.

"All of you heard Pat Bentley's message that night," he said. "Undoubtedly you remember it in detail. Now I want your attention —"

He took the record, moved to a portable phonograph which Havens had also set up. Placing the disc on it, he wound the machine.

"Bentley," Van said, his voice grim, "was a news commentator for Mr. Havens before he became a transport pilot. He covered important air news, mostly. Because he was in great demand, many of his news broadcasts were recorded by the studio, as a matter of course. This is one such record which was sold to a limited public. Bentley had drawn the assignment to cover the arrival of the dirigible *Hindenburg*. As usual, his broadcast from Lakehurst was recorded, without any inkling of how sensational it was to become."

He placed the needle on the whirling record. Immediately a youthful, crisp voice-the voice of Pat Bentley-filled the silent office.

"Well, folks, Germany's pride of the air is just coming into sight now. In the twilight she's been maneuvering around to avoid storms-But they're nosing her down now —"

The voice went on, calm and crisp, giving a routine news broadcast. Describing the crowds. The big ship coming down. Guy-ropes dropping as she maneuvered towards the mooring mast and —

It came then! The phonograph itself seemed to shake with a sudden reverberating sound, followed by a roaring crackle. And then, suddenly frenzied with amazement and horror, came Bentley's voice:

"She's burning! She's burning!" Hysterically came the blurted words. "Fire-it's broken out-the whole ship's burning like so much paper!" The crackle of flames, the scream now of trapped passengers so close overhead.

"God, she's going down! She's going to crash! The fire's creeping up —I can feel the heat now-getting worse-worse! No hope! Going to crash!" A rending, terrific impact. "She's hit-Folks, forgive me if I can hardly speak-This is the most ghastly thing I've ever witnessed-Wait, I must go and see if I can help in the rescue —"

Van stopped the record there.

The four radio men were standing frozen, stupefied. At the words, "She's burning!" all had gone rigid, as if again they were back in the radio room where they had heard those words before. But at the concluding phrases they were apparently feeling the shock of realization.

"Why," one of them blurted, "those are the same words-that one part there! The same, exactly!"

"What can this mean?" Harvey demanded hoarsely.

"It means," the Phantom clipped, "that the plane that cracked on the plateau did not catch fire in the sky at all. In some way-how I do not yet know-Bentley and his co-pilot were persuaded to leave the radio beam, and to land on that Catskill plateau, where I found wheel-tracks that proved the ship had landed intact.

"The message you heard from Bentley was this phonograph record, played by the criminal or his henchmen in the shack, when somehow Bentley himself was cut off from the air. The record was literally made to order for the criminal's scheme. Or rather it probably inspired the basic idea for the whole thing!"

"But," Harvey cried, "the plane did burn!"

"Yes." Van's eyes were slits. "After it had landed, the criminals burned it on the ground — deliberately cremating its occupants, who must have been first rendered helpless or perhaps they might have been drugged into total unconsciousness."

"Good God!" Havens gave that horrified exclamation. "Of all the fiendish —"

"Yes, it's fiendish," Van agreed. "And we're dealing with a criminal who hasn't stopped there, one who is violating every code of law and humaneness. I intend to find that criminal —"

He turned to Harvey. "Mr. Harvey, there's one point about that airplane crash that I haven't yet brought to light. I happen to know that the plane was carrying a great deal of Empire and Southwest stock as well as Garth and Truesdale, two of the railway's most valuable technicians.

"That, as you can readily see, virtually makes that plane more valuable to the railway than to your own lines. So that its doom and the looting of the stock further helped cripple the Empire and Southwest."

Harvey had gone rigid, his eyes flaming.

"What do you mean? What are you getting at?"

"According to Garrison and the rest, you have long been trying to buy out that railway at the cheapest possible price. I am not accusing you. I am just stating your rather delicate position in this matter."

Harvey had abruptly paled. "I don't deny I've tried to buy them out-but I wanted to run the railroad in conjunction with my planes, not wipe it out! Good Lord, how can you think that I —Why, no man is more anxious than I am to see the guilty party behind this horrible crime brought to justice."

Chapter XIV
Rendezvous

Frank Havens drove the Phantom back to New York. "Van," Havens demanded, as they went through the Holland Tunnel, "there's one thing I still can't understand about that air wreck. How did you know where to have them locate it?"

"Through Pat Bentley," Van said simply, and at last gave the information he had withheld. As Havens's knuckles went white on the steering wheel, he told the story of that unidentified corpse he had found in the street.

"And, so that this wouldn't be learned," he concluded, "they were going to put Bentley's buttons and watch on me when they burned me!"

"But why did Bentley come to New York, Van, after calling the inspector at Mulford?" Havens demanded. "Why didn't he tell what he knew when he did call?"

"Because," said Van, his face set and hard, "he probably knew this was something of staggering momentousness. Frank, I'm convinced he wanted to come to you, his old boss who he knew could get the Phantom. And because I happen to live on Park Avenue, the irony of Fate brought him to my door."

His eyes went grim with a fierce purpose which drove the fatigue, the pain of the burns he still felt from his lithe body.

"I'm going to see that he didn't come to my door in vain, Frank!" he promised.

The two men finished the journey in silence —

It was close to another dawn.

Once more disguised, the Phantom paced in the shadow of buildings on West End Avenue, directly opposite the private sanitarium where he had learned Garrison was still staying, despite the murder of Ware that had occurred there.

Before coming here, Van had been busy at his laboratory. That bit of ore-like substance he had found in the fireproof briefcase at the plane had gone through an intensive analysis. The results had not been definite, because the piece was too small to prove what Van suspected. Later he meant to make further tests.

As he paced, his eyes gleamed with hope. He flicked up his wrist-watch. A few minutes more, now, according to the discreet inquiries he had made previously.

He passed those minutes patiently with that unflagging patience that he could muster in his grim investigations.

Then, suddenly, his muscles rippled with quick preparation for movement.

An oblong of light slanted down the small stoop as the front door of the sanitarium opened. Nurse Shirley Keenan, a dark cape thrown over her white uniform, came out on her serviceable-heeled white shoes. It was the hour when she was off her night shift, permitted to go home or stay at the sanitarium for sleep.

No sooner had she appeared than Van moved like a shadow. Down the block to a small parked Chevrolet coupe on his own side of the street.

He had already made sure, by checking the license, that the coupe was owned by Shirley Keenan. And he had also picked open the lock of its rumble seat.

He had waited only to make sure the nurse was heading for the car. Before she or any passers-by could possibly have seen the movement, Van lifted the rumble seat, and climbed in, doubling his lithe body on the floor, pulling the cover over him.

As he settled in the cramped space, he heard her climb in. The door slammed. There came the whine of the self-starter, the cold bark of the motor.

The car was moving. Once or twice Van dared to raise the lid a little. Not so far that she might see it in the rear-view mirror, but far enough to watch the progress of the car.

It was heading down West End Avenue.

Nurse Keenan drove fast, though she heeded the few traffic lights still on at this hour. Quickly West End Avenue changed from an exclusive residential section to a gloomy street where freight trains ran, Eleventh Avenue or, as it was called because of all the accidents that had occurred here, "Death Avenue."

Presently, near the freight yards where many parallel tracks crossed the avenue, the Chevrolet came to a stop, was parked at the curb.

His body cramped from the ride, Van waited until he heard the nurse getting out, heard her heels clicking across cobblestones.

Then quickly he lifted the rumble seat, his body gratefully uncoiling, and leaped soundlessly to the pavement.

The caped figure of the nurse was moving straight into the freight yard, unnoticed by a watchman some distance away. A strange place for a private nurse on her off hour to be going, Van thought tightly.

Strange, yet not irrelevant. This was also part of the Empire and Southwest's spur. Its freight division.

To a desolately dark portion of the tracks the girl moved, to freight cars obviously long since abandoned, and left here on rusty tracks to decay.

Then, incredibly, she climbed into the open, slide door of one of those abandoned cars!

Van did not follow her to that door.

Instead he slipped around to the one which was also open. Cautiously he peered into the car.

A dim light flickered inside the musty, empty car interior. The nurse stood by that light, as if waiting. And a change seemed to have come over her. Her face was hard, her eyes cold, calculating.

She reached beneath her cape, pulled out a small flat automatic; held it, as if prepared.

Van ducked low as he heard a heavy step, a low whistle, thrice repeated.

He lifted his head again when he realized the step came from the other side of the car. From his door he peered through, to see a shadowy, capped figure climbing into the train.

The girl, gripping her gun, stood tense, challenging, as the man came into the light. Van could not see his face. All he could see was that the man was large of build, and moved agilely. Also he could see that the man's clothes were dusty.

The Phantom knew, however, that he hadn't seen this man before.

"Hello, Frenchy," the nurse greeted.

The man, whose hands were in his pockets as he swaggered toward her, barked challengingly, with a Gallic accent:

"What is zis? You I do not know!"

"Sure you do."

The nurse stepped forward. She swept off her cap. And then, as she removed hairpins, her blond hair also came off!

Wavy red locks were revealed. That alone changed her whole aspect.

Crouched at the door, a comprehensive light was in the Phantom's slitted eyes. His keen deductions had again been correct.

"Ah, it is indeed Mademoiselle Keety," came in relieved tones from Frenchy.

Kitty! The gun moll who had brought orders from the criminal for the Phantom's death! Kitty, leading a dual life, playing a female Jekyll-Hyde role, showing a mastery of disguise which almost rivaled the Phantom's own.

But clever women could do that sort of thing. Makeup was part of their everyday routine. Rouge, lipstick of varying shades, artfully applied to suit varying chosen roles could change almost any woman into another personality, totally different from her natural self.

She had almost completely fooled the Phantom. He had not recognized her as Nurse Keenan at the plateau. Not until he had seen her hands had he even guessed her identity.

He glanced at the shoes she wore-nurse's shoes she had to keep whitened. Some of that stuff must have clung to her fingers despite a thorough hand washing. She had brought it on her fingers to the plateau.

A nurse? This cold, criminal-minded woman? Garrison's private nurse. Now it was clear who had tipped off the criminal Tycoon about the Phantom's identity!

But that still did not answer the question-was the murderer one of the people in the hospital, or an outsider?

But though these thoughts flitted instantaneously through Van's brain, primarily his attention was on the gun moll and "Frenchy." He could only see the man's dust-covered back now.

"Well, I am arrive," Frenchy was saying. "An' I think I should receive, yes, more cut of ze money. Ze boss he does not know eet is difficul'. More and more police they send against us down there."

Kitty flung back her head and laughed contemptuously.

"And I thought you were a tough egg-you, claiming to be an apache! Listen, Frenchy! You better not beef to the Tycoon! He might get sore, and then he could sort of tip off the French coppers that he knows where they can nab Jacques Barac, who ran away from the-What d'you call that meat-chopper?"

"The guillotine!" Deadly fear was in the words. Van could see the broad back tremble. "Dieu, he would not squeal on me, ze Tycoon?"

"Not if you play ball! But I ain't talkin' for him! I got a message for you, that's all! Tonight, at six o'clock, you go to the corner of West Broadway and Bleecker Street, uptown side, and —" Rapidly she described the spot. "You'll be picked up there."

The girl made a gesture to show that she had finished the interview. She was replacing her wig and cap, powdering her face as she held a small compact.

"Go the way you came," she instructed Frenchy.

She extinguished the lamp. Then Van crouched suddenly back from the doorway, for she came to his side of the freight car, jumped agilely to the ground.

She passed within feet of the Phantom, unconscious of his nearness. She headed for her car, as Frenchy who had climbed out the other side of the freight car started away in a different direction.

The Phantom reached a quick decision. He had the girl spotted now; knew her role of nurse in the sanitarium. He was more interested, just now, in Frenchy!

Stealthily he slid around the freight car. The back of the French apache was disappearing across the yards.

Van followed. His plan was formulating swiftly. Capture Frenchy-secretly. Make up as the French thug and take his place at that West Broadway rendezvous.

Glancing back to Eleventh Avenue as he gained on his quarry now, the Phantom saw a car moving off. The girl was probably returning to the hospital.

Van drew out his Colt —a new one replacing that he had lost to the gangsters. No one was in sight, though a train of freight cars was backing slowly out of the yard, on a track close ahead.

In the darkness, the Phantom swiftly closed behind Frenchy.

And then some sixth sense-for certainly Van made no sound on his soft-soled shoes-must have warned the foreign thug. Of a sudden he whirled. In the darkness Van only saw his eyes-glowing dark eyes.

"All right!" Van said crisply, his voice low but menacing. "Put your hands up, Frenchy!"

With a shrill cry, the Frenchman leaped wildly at Van.

The Phantom could have shot him dead then, but he wanted the man alive. He brought his gun down on the capped head, hoping to stun Frenchy. But the cap was heavily padded, and evidently the apache's skull was thick!

The next instant a human cyclone struck Van. He knew how the apaches fought-with hands, feet, teeth-anything that could punish and do damage! And here was a taste of it.

The Phantom managed to shove his gun into his coat freeing both hands to grapple with the desperate thug. Then his powerful arms were getting a grip on Frenchy, tying up that windmill of fists and feet.

Frenchy suddenly lurched away. Something glittered in his hand. A knife! With desperate skill, he was maneuvering its deadly point toward Van's chest.

Both were wrestling across the tracks now. With fresh alarm, Van saw a glowing red light moving towards them-the freight train that was backing out! He grabbed at the knife, twisting it aside. Even as he was doubling his fist to hurl a blow at Frenchy's jaw the apache, in his effort to retrieve the knife, gave a mighty backward lurch.

It pulled both man and knife from Van's grip, sent him staggering to the middle of the track. "Look out!" Van cried, his heart stopping.

But it happened before he could prevent it; before the brakeman on the rear car could stop it either.

Though moving with fairly slow speed the train loomed over Frenchy like a Juggernaut. Half off balance, he was struck down by the push of the freight car bumper.

He screamed once as he fell —a short, horrible scream, cut off like a phonograph record. Then the train was rolling over him, the heavy steel wheels rumbling.

Minutes later, the Phantom saw police gathering around a mangled, bloody mass of flesh and bone and torn clothing. All that was left of Frenchy. The steel wheels had ground his body to a pulp before they could be stopped.

And Van's eyes were grim.

Frenchy had died despite his efforts to keep him alive-and Van had not even seen his face; would never see it now!

It was already daybreak. In less than twelve hours, Frenchy's rendezvous was scheduled.

Chapter XV
A Perilous Chance

Half of those hours had passed when the Phantom, once more in the great laboratory of "Doctor Bendix," was making ready for the most perilous experiment of his entire career in crime-detection.

On a table, he had laid sheaves of paper. One was a cablegram. The others were still-damp pictures which had been sent by the Bartlane wireless photo process.

Both had come from France, from the headquarters of the famous *Surete,* in Paris. Havens had handled the telephoto with the facilities of his papers.

During his visit to Havens, however, the Phantom had received another set-back in his plans.

He had ordered the police to go quietly to the Ferris Sanitarium, and secretly arrest Nurse Keenan. But evidently some woman's intuition had told her that the law was on her trail, for she had vanished completely, leaving Garrison without a nurse. Van had given a description of her as Kitty, the gun moll, and a general alarm was out for her.

Grim-eyed, the Phantom gave his attention now to the wireless photos. A vague, smudgy face peered from them. It had not taken him long to decide the pictures were useless to him. Evidently they had not been good pictures, to begin with. The transmission had made them more vague.

He picked up the long cablegram. It read:

TO THE PHANTOM

JACQUES BARAC ALIAS L'APACHE MORT ALIAS FRENCHY WANTED AS FUGITIVE FROM JUSTICE CONDEMNED TO GUILLO-TINE STOP THE BERTILLON MEASUREMENTS OF THIS CRIMINAL FOLLOW

Then followed detailed numbers and signifying letters. The anthropometric system of French criminal identifications.

Van drew out an immense drawing board, on which paper was fastened with thumb tacks. He divided it, by rule and T-square, into several squares, all numbered.

Then he set to work. His long study of the methods of the French Secret Police gave him a full understanding of the system by which, from bone measurements which could not change, they reproduced likenesses of wanted criminals.

Every bone structure of the face, from forehead to chin, was identified as a "type," marked by a number, which Van found in his book on the subject. The face itself was divided into numbered squares, representing these parts.

From the guiding numbers of the cable, and his own book on the subjects, Van began to fill in those squares.

Slowly, parts of a face took life-size shape. A cruel face with high cheek bones, small, wide-apart eyes, a sharp, hooked nose, a thick-lipped but evil mouth, and a receding chin.

Van looked at the cable:

COMPLEXION SWARTHY STOP HAIR CHESTNUT COARSELY THICK

Finished with his work at the drawing board, Van carried the drawing with its measurements into the alcove dressing room. Here he arranged not the daylight lamp, but a powerful flood-light, for he was making up for night, not for day. Then, with only the drawing he had made, with bone structure measurements as his model, he set to work.

The high cheek bones first. Bits of rubber, shoved under his gums, upward, held by small wire clamps. The sharp nose then. A wire pincer over his own nose; flesh-colored clay added.

Then a cream dye to give the swarthy complexion; a special preparation to coarsen his own hair before he used another dye to bring it to the right color.

In his mirror a replica of the face in the drawing was slowly but definitely taking shape.

Was it the face of Frenchy? Despite his faith in the Bertillon method, Van could not be certain.

"But I've got to chance it!" he gritted.

With a swift movement he swept aside the curtain of his replete clothes wardrobe. He had at least seen Frenchy's suit. It was not difficult to find a suit of somewhat similar material. He put it on.

FRENCHY HAD CARRIED A KNIFE-no gun had been found on him. Van moved to a closet, unlocked it. A small arsenal containing every conceivable weapon from a Malay *kris* to a Western derringer gleamed before him. He selected a knife of the type Frenchy had drawn, shoved it into his belt. But he also pocketed a .38 automatic.

Nor was he finished yet.

Moving to his full length mirrors he walked up and down, imitating the way he had seen Frenchy walk. He made gestures that Frenchy had made while the apache had been talking.

He moved to a Dictaphone, he began to speak into it, phrases that Frenchy had spoken; mimicking the man's accents. "Ah, Mademoiselle Keety-Well I am arrive —*Dieu,* he would not squeal on me, ze Tycoon!"

He played the record back, listened to it with critical appraisal. For a full hour he practiced before he was satisfied.

Then, over the private wire which ran straight from here to the *Clarion* Building, he called Frank Havens.

"Any new developments?" he demanded.

"Yes, Van!" the publisher announced tensely. "You remember Leland Sprague? The surveyor who found the body of Brooks the other night? Well, Strickland has reported him missing from his home. Fears something happened to him!"

Van's eyes went grim. Had the Tycoon struck again?

"And another thing, Van. The first autopsies on some of those airplane victims were made. There was a heavy morphine content in the stomach of each as well as food and caffeine. It begins to look as if they were drugged before being killed!"

"Have any of the bodies been identified as Max Garth's?" Van asked.

"No, though most of them have been identified. No sign of Garth's body, nor that of Nancy Clay, the stewardess-By the way, Van, I have those maps you asked for from the Department of Commerce. The maps of the air-field in Nevada that group of scientists drew up for the Government."

"Good! Send them over here to my laboratory any time, though I don't know just when I'll get at them."

"What are you doing now?" Havens asked anxiously.

Van spoke grimly. "I'm about to experiment with the late Monsieur Bertillon's famous system. An experiment by which I hope to get still closer to this Tycoon!"

* * *

West Broadway and Bleecker Street at its least crowded hour.

Elevated trains rumbling overhead. And, on the northwest corner, moving about furtively as if he had an eye out for the police, a swarthy-faced, sharp-nosed man, plainly Gallic.

The Phantom had come on the dot at the scheduled time. Now he waited, his heart pounding with cold suspense.

So smoothly did the dark sedan slide up to the curb that at first, even alert, he scarcely noticed it. Then he saw the rear door open, heard a low whistle.

The crucial moment had come.

With a swaggering walk, Van approached the car. He climbed in confidently.

He found himself sitting down next to the burly Ape. At the other window, Slick, now wearing his pearl-grey slouch hat over his patent-leather hair, leaned forward. The movement showed that distinguishing scar.

"Okay, Luke!" Slick ordered.

The thin, angular-faced thug was at the wheel. He promptly started the car, sent it back into traffic.

"How's your eye-sight, Frenchy?" Slick asked the question sharply.

For a brief moment he pondered that. Then he laughed shrilly, speaking for the first time. "Eet is ver' good. Why?"

"Because," said Slick, "you ain't gonna be using it for a little while-Now hold still, I got my gat on you, and Ape here is handy with his mitts!"

For a moment Van felt his arduously built-up plans crumbling about him. Then, as a heavy cloth was brought roughly over his eyes by Ape and securely fastened, the moment passed.

For Slick said: "You savvy, we ain't taken any chances. You're still a new guy to us, even if you have been workin' in the other territory, and we've all seen you."

Van sat still. The blindfold, which Slick himself reached over to adjust, fully obliterated his vision. He did not try to maneuver it. He was playing a precarious enough part and must do nothing suspicious.

Thus far he seemed to be getting by. They had seen the real Frenchy whom he had never seen, yet his disguise seemed to have passed their inspection.

The car rolled on. Now and then Van could tell that it was stopping in traffic, or turning, but he could not gauge its course. Once he heard a sound in the rushing wind as of the sides of a bridge passing; he could sense water. But he wasn't sure what bridge it was.

Then the car suddenly gathered speed, rolled smoothly, rapidly. An open road now, doubtless.

For a long period the journey continued. Another turn, then the car began to jounce roughly, violently, making slower progress.

Then at last it came to a stop.

Instantly the blindfold was taken from Van's face, and he was glad his makeup had been put on solidly enough not to be affected by it.

With the others he climbed out of the car, in night which was pitch dark. But with his blindfold accustomed eyes he could see clearly.

The trees of a heavy woods rose darkly on every side. The Phantom and his underworld companions were standing on a clearing amid those trees, on a lawn where reared a dark, stone mansion.

What was the location of this house Van could not guess. Nor did he have much opportunity to study its exterior.

"Come on, Frenchy," Slick said. "We ain't got much time."

With Ape walking behind in his loping gait, all moved to the front door of the house. Slick pressed a bell-button, but apparently the bell gave no sound. Waiting only a moment he took out a key and opened the front door.

They came directly into a large foyer. A heavy oak door was opposite them, closed. The foyer was dimly lighted, the furniture covered with shrouding cloth.

And at once Van became aware of an evil atmosphere in this place —a sense of chill menace.

"Wait!" commanded Slick.

He walked across the foyer to that heavy door; rapped on it three times.

There was a click, as of a lock being turned. Slick opened the door, slid quickly through it, closing it before Van could glimpse the room beyond.

Minutes passed. No sound came from the closed-off room. Ape stood patiently, rolling a cigarette with his pawlike hands. Luke paced the floor. Another gangster came in then and Van recognized the twisty-faced man as Maxie.

"Say! Look who's here!" Maxie exclaimed. "If it ain't Frenchy! Hope you brought good news."

"Stow it!" Luke said gruffly. "No questions or talking here. You know the rules, Maxie."

Silence again in the foyer.

Then once more the oak door opened. Slick came out. He looked awed, yet a trifle disappointed, and he wheezed as if he were cold. His eyes flashed to Maxie.

"Come on, you! We ain't gonna go on this job. The boss wants us to wait around for orders." He nodded to "Frenchy."

"Go in—Ape, you stay with Luke. Both o' you wait for Frenchy."

Chapter XVI
The Ice Chamber

As Slick and Maxie moved for the front door, Van walked unhesitatingly to the door of oak and the inner room. He tried the knob. The door was unlocked. His nerves steeled, he pulled it open, entered.

On its own spring the door closed behind him.

He found himself in a large, brightly lighted oblong chamber, with bare walls. Though there were no visible signs of ventilation, the air seemed fresh. Also it was strangely cold, bringing an instant chill to his body.

Though his senses registered these things, his real attention was immediately drawn, as if magnetically, to the far end of this strange room.

In the metal wall was a small square window of heavy glass. And as Van walked forward in the bright light which was challenging every line of his makeup, he discerned a face in that window.

A crazy grotesquerie of a face. Distorted as some face in an amusement park's sideshow mirror. Shimmery features which had a ghastly aspect.

But the Phantom realized, as he looked at that grotesque visage, that the glass of the window had probably been made with some deliberate imperfection to cause that distortion.

"All right, Frenchy! Stand where you are!"

From a camouflaged microphone in the glass the voice, a strange ghostly whisper which nevertheless filled the bare-walled room, rapped out the command. At the same time, the air seemed to grow colder-uncomfortably colder.

The Phantom came to a stop some twelve feet from that window.

"Well, Frenchy, now you meet me personally." The distorted features shimmered eerily. "I am your boss-the Tycoon!"

Van had all he could do to conceal the surge of hate and rage that flamed through his every fiber. His hand itched to whip out his gun. Behind that distorting window stood the master criminal he had sought on a trail of blood and slaughter.

Twelve feet apart that criminal and the greatest living detective faced one another. But the Phantom knew that as far as coming to vital grips with the criminal went, that distance might as well have been miles instead of feet.

He had seen the invulnerable position of the Tycoon. Not only was the wall metal, the glass undoubtedly bullet-proof, but the criminal had another, even better protection.

This big, bare chamber outside the window was obviously air-conditioned. And from behind that window, the criminal himself operated the air-conditioning power. His making the room colder when he had wanted "Frenchy" to halt had been a warning.

Cleverly hidden vents near the ceiling were letting that cold air in. Unquestionably, if the criminal willed, he could turn that air to freezing point, could make it fatal for any human, while in his segregated chamber the Tycoon could remain comfortable and safe.

But who was he? In his Gallic pose, Van peered hard at that shimmery, grotesque face in the window.

An eerie chuckle sounded from the microphone then.

"I am sorry you cannot see me as clearly as I can see you," came the voice of the Tycoon.

Van was glad then that he had not relaxed playing his role to perfection, in every posture. That glass must have clear places in it, through which the criminal peered, saw him out here in the bright light, watched his every move.

"And now, Frenchy, to business. My time is valuable. It is not often I give it to anyone. Soon all will realize my position!" The whisper rose in gloating triumph. "They will pay tribute to me in millions-millions. You know that, do you not, Frenchy?"

"*But* oui, I know eet!"

It was the first time Van had spoken in this eerie place. And even as he spoke, he was grimly wondering what mad scheme of power and wealth this diabolical criminal had. There was a ghastly confidence in the man's egotistical boasting.

"And that brings me to your work, Frenchy." The eerie, whispery voice changed in tone. "I am not completely satisfied with the results you and your mob have been getting in-your territory. Up here, my men have worked smoothly and tirelessly. You used to give me more action! What is the matter?"

Even as he puzzled over this speech, the Phantom's retentive memory leaped suddenly into the gap of his unconnected thoughts. He took a long shot, and quoted almost verbatim words he had heard the real Frenchy speak. Even though he knew they were perilous words, he had to make his role convincing.

"Eet is ver' difficult, *Monsieur* Tycoon. Ze police zey make theengs hot. I do not weesh to complain, but ze cut of ze money—"

"Ah, so that's it?"

The whisper had become a tigerish purr. And significantly, the air in the room grew still colder. With alarming rapidity. Van felt goose-flesh pimple his body as almost Arctic air came rushing through the vents.

"Oh, eet ees cold! Please, *Monsieur* Boss—I do not mean to offend."

"No, you could not be that foolish. That is why I shall pass over your words, and forget them. And perhaps you will yet redeem yourself. I am going to send you back now, along with two of the boys who will show you how we operate up here! If you can help them, so much the better. This is an important job, and I am taking no chances!"

As he spoke, Van noticed the temperature of the room was no longer dropping. But the air remained uncomfortably cold, refrigerated. And it was at that very moment that Van became aware of a sensation that filled him with sudden alarm. The skin of his face, under his makeup, was becoming rigid, painfully taut!

He knew, with a sharp clutch at his heart, what was happening. His makeup could have stood heat; even blistering heat. But he had not expected to find himself in icy coldness!

His makeup was stiffening in that cold. The cream dyes were shrinking as they congealed! The fixed temperature was doing its work! As he stood there he could feel that artificial face changing, contracting, beginning to pull out of shape!

He knew the criminal's eyes were watching that face. In another moment the would Tycoon see. Van would be betrayed! And something told him that if he were, he would never get as far as that oak-paneled, air-tight door with its lock apparently operated from behind the criminal's window.

In that perilous instant, with the contraction starting to distort his face, Van's mind raced. Some loophole, some escape—

Then swift inspiration came.

With a feigned gasp the Phantom let his knees go limp. He dropped to the floor of the icy room as if passing out from the effects of the icy air. It had, indeed, brought lassitude to his body.

He fell forward, so that he could put one hand to his face to shield it and warm it at the same time.

"Ah-too much for my warmblooded apache friend?" The criminal behind the glass chuckled. And the air suddenly grew warmer. Van stirred. If only he could get a chance to come to grips with that fiend!

A bell clanged, somewhere outside the oaken door. The lock clicked and Ape, with the tall, angular-faced Luke came in, with drawn guns.

"Take Frenchy out of here-and go on with the job!" came the eerie whisper. It seemed to recede as if sinking.

And the moment after Ape had "helped" Van to his feet, the grotesque face disappeared from the window.

"Come on!" Luke said, shivering. "It's damn cold in here. An' we just about got time to make it."

They were pulling Van along to the open oak door. The Phantom did not resist, nor try any false moves. The criminal leader was still safely out of reach, and this mission to which the Tycoon had assigned him was going to be vital. It seemed his best lead now.

His companions led him through the empty foyer, thence out into the tree-shrouded grounds, into the dark night. Van heard the muffled purr of a high-powered auto motor, somewhere in the rear of the house. The Tycoon-driving away?

In vain the Phantom tried to guess his surroundings as they moved across the soggy, muddy grass. At least it didn't seem they were going to blindfold him now. He should find out before long where this eerie house was located.

Then, suddenly, he suppressed a sharp intake of breath.

They had reached a turn. And, nestled in a bay of trees, a silvery cabin monoplane loomed into view, squatting like a huge bird with outspread wings.

A modern Fairchild it was, Van saw at once. Luke stepped forward with an authoritative air. The tall gunman opened the cabin door, stepped in, reaching for the dashboard. Then he hurried around to the self-starter.

The starter moaned. Its moan was drowned in the sudden staccato burst of the Wright engine coming to life, as the propeller whirled.

Luke, obviously a trained pilot, was already in the front seat, at the stick. He had turned on the cabin lights.

Ape's huge figure climbed in next, then Van followed. There were two seats behind the pilot, opposite one another. Ape took one. Van took the other, pulling the door closed at a command.

The motor scaled up and down, warming. Then the plane lurched forward. Expertly, Luke taxied the ship across the wide clearing, headed it into the wind. A rush of gathering speed, then the sudden smooth lift as the monoplane took the air.

The Phantom looked covertly from his window as the dark ground dropped away.

He saw the dark mansion, the woods, but they looked vague because the lights in the cabin lessened visibility outside.

The plane was climbing in a slow circular course. And before Van's keen eyes could get a clearer view of the mysterious locale they had left the place behind and low-hanging cloud-wisps engulfed the ship. Luke was watching his dashboard instruments, flying by them. Nor could Van see them clearly from his seat, though he could hear the buzz of the radio compass.

Vaporish mists wisped past the windows. Then clear starlight. Luke was above the clouds.

Chapter XVII
Sky Ride

Unquestionably, a full hour went by with no conversation in the throbbing, coursing plane. Luke silently guided the controls. Ape settled back in his seat, in an attitude of relaxation. The Phantom was still wondering from where they had taken off, and where they were headed.

Once his glance had gone down covertly to his shoes. He noted that they were caked with mud from the grounds over which he had walked. Peculiar, greyish mud.

Unobtrusively Van managed to scrape some of that mud off with a bit of match-box from his pocket, and to shove the folded cardboard away. Once before a pair of shoes had aided him-the white shoes of "Nurse Keenan."

A sudden gap appeared in the cloud-vapors through which the ship was coursing and, glancing through the window, Van caught a glimpse of the dark relief-map earth below. Rough terrain, with dark hillocks that were growing to mountain ranges! Somewhere off to the right the faint tentacle of a beacon-light darted into the sky.

"Where are we, Luke?" Ape asked gruffly. "Jersey?"

Luke spoke without turning. "Cripes, we passed outa Jersey ten minutes ago. We're crossin' Pennsy now. And I hope the Tycoon gave us plenty of fuel for this trip so's we can make it on the exact time he planned!"

As time went on, Van Loan learned that he was being taken on no small "hop." The plane was racing across the continent! Flying on a steady, southwesterly course while Luke, who Van realized was not only an expert pilot but a tireless one, guided it by the regular air-beacons and radio beams.

The darkness of the night deepened as the ship winged in and out of clouds. Once it "detoured" to avoid a storm area which showed black in the sky, an area that was being announced by the radio operator of the Pittsburgh airport.

Ape's big head was lolled back now. The huge thug dozed off, and his snores rose beneath the engine's throb. But Luke continued to guide the controls in silence.

The Phantom's mind was working at top speed. With each hour he was being flown further from New York; from the scene of his investigations. Should he try to wrest control of this ship-capture these two thugs and fly back? He could do it, with Ape snoring, and with Luke concentrating on the controls.

But he didn't make such a move. The Tycoon had said, "an important job," and the Phantom must learn what that job was. He must know why this plane was making such a long trip.

And so he, too, pretended to relax while the night dragged on. Actually, though, he was wide awake, alert to every change in their course, to every buzz of the radio compass.

He knew when they were passing over Ohio. The winding silver ribbon that was the Ohio River gave him his bearings. Ohio-then Indiana, stretching its flat plains below.

Ape woke up as they winged over Illinois. The big thug reached into a compartment and produced sandwiches and a thermos bottle of coffee. He took a greedy share of both, passed them next to Luke who used one hand to drink and eat. "Frenchy" was then offered his share-and the Phantom partook of this felon's meal, knowing his body must have nourishment to maintain its energy.

When the grey dawn seeped across the sky, and the sun rose red behind the speeding plane, Missouri was spread out below.

Full morning found them flying over Kansas, over dusty flatlands.

Then, just as Van was wondering whether this flight was going to cross the whole continent, Luke twisted his expressionless face over his shoulder and spoke. In his tone was the triumph lacking in his features.

"We've hit the schedule to the dot, guys! Now if the boss was right —"

As he spoke he was easing the joy-stick forward. The plane dipped, began a long descent over the Kansas landscape-over the Southwest state to which Van had flown so far in company with two underworld thugs.

The earth loomed beneath the descending ship. Dusty fields, meadows, trees. And then Van saw twin, glistening lines growing into distinctness-lines which cut across that landscape.

Railroad tracks!

Luke was following them with the speeding plane, having leveled it at low altitude. For a long period the Fairchild sped on a parallel over those glistening lines.

Again Luke twisted his head around to speak.

"Be ready, Ape. Ought to be comin' in sight now!"

Instantly Ape was fully awake, his eyes gleaming with evil anticipation. He reached beneath his seat and Van, heart tightening, watched him pull out a wooden box he had already noticed there.

Pear-shaped, steel-encased missiles gleamed in that box. Grenades!

"You can help with the pineapples, Frenchy!" Ape said, grinning ghoulishly. "You oughta know the lay down these parts!"

A shout suddenly broke from Luke. The Fairchild abruptly slanted steeply, rushing down a hill of space with roaring speed.

"There she is!" Luke cried.

Van looked. His eyes widened.

On the track below and ahead, a long, glistening train had loomed. A streamlined train, racing along those rails like a graceful, silvery bullet! Obviously one of the latest Diesel-engined trains. It moved effortlessly, smokelessly. Ape had opened the window beside him, ignoring the rush of wind. The big thug lifted one of the "pineapples."

Closer loomed the train which, despite its speed, was far slower than the down-rushing airplane.

So this was the grim objective which had brought these thugs way to Kansas! They were diving on a streamlined train —a train full of people! Diving with murderous intent!

Ape was taking aim with the bomb now as the plane, swooping low over the rounded roof of the train, banked to give him a perfect throwing range.

And in that instant, Van knew that he must act. Role or no role, he could not sit idly by and watch an act of such devilish destruction! Though for almost twelve hours he had withheld himself from any action, he could do so no longer.

Ape's arm came back to take aim with the bomb-and the Phantom pushed out of his seat, sideward. He lunged with his shoulders against Ape's arm, cleverly blocking it in its poised position.

Ape cursed. "Hey, what the hell's the matter with you, Frenchy?"

"Ze lurch, it threw me," Van explained quickly.

The plane had slithered on past the gleaming, streamlined train, was banking vertically to swoop anew.

"Get over it, Luke!" Ape growled. "I'll finish it right!"

Again the train was beneath them. Ape once more aimed the pineapple. And again the Phantom deliberately lurched. This time he could not block the throw but he delayed it. The plane had slithered past the train and over a field before Ape could let go with the grenade.

A geyser of brief flame, followed by the slower-traveling concussion, shot out of the empty field-safely to one side and behind the train.

Ape growled a curse at this second apparent clumsiness which had spoiled his aim. But another cold voice suddenly snapped out like a whip. Luke's voice.

"I saw that, Frenchy! You did it on purpose! Trying to ball up the works, eh?" The pilot, holding the plane in a climb, was looking back, his hard, expressionless eyes giving his face a deadly aspect. "Say, no wonder the boss didn't trust you too much! If you think you're gonna pull a doublecross —"

With a snarl, with that quickness by which an underworld felon could change at once from comrade to deadly foe, Luke whipped out an automatic, snaked it around.

The Phantom threw all pretense aside then. Gritting an oath, he catapulted forward. His hand caught the pilot's gun arm. His other hand, balled into a fist, swung in a short but terrific jab to Luke's angular jaw.

The pilot gasped, slumped; out for the instant. The plane leveled into neutral by its own stabilizer.

A growl of enraged comprehension came from Ape then. The big man had turned from the window, was lurching forward, his head low to avoid the ceiling. And his big hands scooped up a tommy gun. Its muzzle swung like a dark cannon-maw at the Phantom.

"You doublecrossin' rat!"

Van had no time to draw his own secreted automatic. The tommy was right in front of his face, ready to blow his head off!

He made one rapid movement-swooped one long arm for the joystick, gave it a crazy yank.

The Fairchild see-sawed drunkenly, standing on one wing tip in midair. Cursing, Ape was thrown off balance, even as the tommy blasted three shots into the cabin ceiling. The plane sideslipped; began to wabble and to lose flying speed.

Its nose dropped sickeningly as the earth came up in a spinning rush. The tracks to one side; the train far ahead.

Ape yelled in alarm as his huge frame slid down the flooring of the steeply tilted ship. Van ignored him now, for the earth was spinning up closer. A fatal crash was imminent.

The Phantom yanked at the stunned pilot to move him from the controls.

And at that very instant Luke came to, began to struggle fiercely, flaying out with both arms, kicking, squirming.

Cramped between chairs, Ape again had the tommy. Somehow, despite the sickening drop of the plane, the huge thug was again aiming that gun at Van.

The Phantom let go of the weak but struggling pilot. This time he managed to get his automatic out. It blazed once in the giddy plane.

Ape's big body slumped over the chairs —a bullet in his brain.

Jagged green trees seemed to leap up at the plane like mammoth teeth. With a mighty heave, Van yanked at the pilot in a final, desperate effort. Even as the ground loomed right below, the Phantom at last cleared the control space, pushing the cursing Luke aside. He slid into the seat, grabbed the stick, found the rubber bars with his feet.

With the skill of an expert flyer, Van struggled with those controls, knowing how slim his chances were of righting the ship. He used the throttle and stick, trying to bring up nose and drooping wing, at the very moment the tree-tops slanted right beneath.

At the last instant he did succeed in getting the plane over a wide road which ran parallel to the railroad tracks. But that was all he could do. He could not get the ship on even keel, nor could he get it to the flatlands on the other side of the tracks. The road came up at a menacing, swinging angle.

Van sat tight, flinging his arms in front of his face, after flicking off the ignition switch. He saw Luke trying to rise, yelled a warning at the thug. Then the crash came!

A rending impact —a shivering moan of twisting metal. Its nose telescoping, the monoplane settled in a wing-buckling heap.

Fortunately, there was no fire, due to Van's quick thought of turning off the ignition. Nor did the "pineapples" aboard explode. By crashing on the road and getting the nose of the plane up as far as possible, Van had avoided an impact that would have blown the whole wrecked plane to bits.

Chapter XVIII
Looted Train

Dazed, shaken, but otherwise unhurt, the Phantom crept through the wrecked cabin. Ape lay on the floor, dead from Van's own bullet. But he was not the only corpse!

With the top of his head horribly crushed, Luke, the angular-faced thug, lay in a gruesome heap. He had made the mistake (an ironic mistake for such a skilled pilot) of trying to stand up when the crash came. A metal roof support had done the rest.

Van got out of the cabin as quickly as he could; out on the road, where he pulled the two corpses. He searched both with lightning speed, took all their possessions.

One article, found on Luke, interested him as he glanced at it quickly. It was a tagged key, marked Piedmont Hotel. Van knew that hotel in New York. It was one of the flashy type of places which gangsters often used as hide-outs, posing as respectable business men.

As Van hastily pocketed the key, a scream of sirens, a raucous roar, came to his ears. Coming down the road were motorcycles, tan-uniformed figures astride them. Kansas State troops —a whole squadron of them! Someone who had seen the plane crash must already have reported it.

Van stood up quickly. Over makeup which, though somewhat marred now, nevertheless still clung to his face, he placed his black silk domino mask.

And then he realized the troopers couldn't have known about the plane. For though none could have failed to see it in the middle of the sunny road, the majority of them did not even stop, but sped past in frantic haste.

The few who braked their machines to a standstill and dismounted were soon staring with surprise at Van's platinum, diamond-studded badge.

"The Phantom!" came husky, ejaculations.

For like the police in every part of this nation, and in every other nation as well, their regulations had reminded them to be on the lookout for that scintillating emblem and its anonymous owner, wherever found.

But the Phantom wasted no time in formalities. Those other motorcycles had sped ahead— something must have —

"What's happened, Sergeant?" he asked one of the troopers. "What were you called out on?"

"Big train wreck-about two miles up, near Emporia," the sergeant answered quickly. "News just phoned in."

The Phantom's heart turned to ice.

A moment later, with one trooper remaining at the crashed plane with its two New York gangster corpses, the remaining motorcycles roared again down the road. And the Phantom sat astride the fender of the careful but speedy-driving sergeant.

Ambulances and local police from Emporia had already reached the wreck when they arrived. In the full morning sun it lay like a ghastly blight upon the landscape.

The streamlined train which Van had saved from an airplane bombing lay toppled over an embankment, its engine telescoped, its silvery cars twisted and bent.

The crew had died, all of them. Most of the passengers still lived, but many of them were horribly maimed, bleeding and groaning as interns rushed with stretchers to pick them up.

From horrified survivors the Phantom learned the facts, and the first thing he learned came with the impact of a blow, though he had already surmised it.

The train belonged to the Empire and Southwest Railway. It had just inaugurated this run, from Topeka to Salt Lake City, Utah.

When the airplane had appeared, no one had known its intent. Its one exploded bomb, well behind and to the side of the train, had not been seen. But as the train proceeded, two closed automobiles had appeared on the parallel road beside it, having turned in from some branch road ahead.

There had been a terrific explosion coming with cataclysmic suddenness. Tracks upturned, and the train derailed. And thugs from those automobiles had looted the baggage car, taking everything of value.

Grim comprehension narrowed the Phantom's eyes. Even in his fierce anger and grief over this ruthless vandalism, he paid unwitting tribute to the devilish cunning of the Tycoon.

In the east, somewhere in or near New York, the criminal leader had planned this crime with utmost thoroughness. It was natural that he could not entirely rely on the plane making the trip on schedule, and doing its work. Out here he must have another mob in contact with him, the mob from which Frenchy had originally come!

They had been on hand, in cars. Even if the plane had succeeded in bombing the train, the local gangsters would still have been needed to loot the wrecked train. They had simply carried out both jobs.

And Van could only console his bitter feelings with the thought that, had he not thwarted the men in the plane the wreck might have taken a greater toll.

In Emporia, where a police chief turned over a private telephone to him, the Phantom put through a long distance call to Frank Havens. The publisher was astounded to hear the Phantom's voice talking from Kansas, when little over twelve hours ago Van had been in New York. But the train wreck was no news to him.

"Yes," he said briefly, "I got it from my correspondent over the wires. I phoned it to Garrison at the sanitarium. It threw him almost into a raving state. He's in debt now, it seems, for backing that streamlined train and its fast run. He relied on it strongly to pull the railroad out of its slump." Havens hesitated for a breath. "But there's something else I have to tell you, Phantom. About Leland Sprague."

Van's heart tightened. "You told me he was missing from his home," he said quickly. "Has anything —"

Havens spoke rapidly. "No—and that's just the point! Sprague showed up at my office about midnight last night. He seemed in a state of utter terror-actually ill, acting wild and queer. Said he felt he needed protection and had come to me in the hope of finding the Phantom. At the same time he denied-pretty vehemently, I thought-that he had been missing at all. Said he'd been home, buried in work, all the hours the police were looking for him. Because he seemed so ill, I insisted on calling my own physician. He took Sprague to the Polyclinic Hospital, saying the man obviously needed rest, if nothing else. Sprague's still there."

The Phantom had listened to this report with narrowing eyes. His apprehension had changed to a sudden sober conjecture. Sprague's absence and return-the timing of them included the hour when Van had seen the mysterious Tycoon at that unknown hide-out.

"Listen, Frank," Van ordered crisply. "Have your doctor make sure that none of Sprague's clothes or other belongings are touched or lost. I want to look into this matter personally when I get back to New York. I'm taking the first plane I can."

* * *

It was not yet midnight when the Phantom opened the multiple-locked door to his secret laboratory in New York's Bronx.

He had already made two visits since his return.

The first he had made with the police-to the Piedmont Hotel. The key he had found on the dead Luke gave him entrance to a room on the twentieth floor. It was deserted, but evidently had been quite recently occupied, not only by Luke, but by others. Clothing was strewn about. So were empty whiskey bottles, glasses, cigarettes.

Van had made a thorough search, taking every item that seemed possible evidence. He had brought them now to his laboratory. Police had been left to guard the hotel room, which had been rented under fictitious names. The Phantom doubted, however, whether any thugs would show up there again.

Before returning to his laboratory Van had hurried to the Polyclinic Hospital. He had seen Leland Sprague there-seen the shock-headed surveyor in a wild, agitated state, his face flushed and feverish, his eyes small-pupiled in their glaring. Talbert, the tall, mustached shoring man, another of the scientists, had also been present, trying to persuade Sprague to remain in the hospital, for Sprague was demanding to go.

Both men had been tight-lipped in the Phantom's presence. Van had learned nothing from them. But he had learned something of significance when he had examined Sprague's clothing, in the privacy of an office. On Sprague's shoes had been two layers of caked, clayish mud. The same mud, Van had seen at once, that he had scraped from his own shoes in the plane, just after leaving the Tycoon's hide-out. Sprague, who had sworn he was not "missing," had been on those grounds!

Havens's doctor, who had attended Sprague, had then said he was unable to tell just what was wrong with the man, but suspected he had recently taken narcotics-cocaine, in all likelihood. Since arriving at the hospital, Sprague had steadfastly refused to submit to thorough examination; above all, he had refused to have a blood test taken.

But the Phantom had come away with some of Sprague's blood nevertheless. The scientist had been scratched on his wrist, which the doctor had bandaged. The bandage was changed, and Van took prompt possession of the old, blood-soaked gauze.

Now, in his laboratory, Van once more put on his smock and set to work.

He gave first attention to the mud he had scraped from his own shoes, and from Sprague's. From his great crime library, came every book on soil he possessed. The dab of mud went under a special geologist's glass, thence through strainers to segregate clay, humus and sand. The Phantom soon analyzed it. He took out a map then, giving in various colors the different types of soil in every locale. He limited himself to a small area of the map, for he knew from the length of that auto journey he had taken blindfolded that the mysterious house couldn't be far out of Manhattan.

At first he saw no green in this area at all.

Then his eyes sharpened. Yes, there was one emerald dab.

Long Island. The only place where soil of this peculiar clayish substance was to be found close to New York City. The clay was present because of the marshy banks of the nearby Sound.

Recalling the immense woods that had surrounded the house, Van took out a map of Long Island, pored over it. When he was finished he had limited the locale to three possible points. Filing this temporarily away in his retentive mind, the Phantom proceeded to his next work.

One of the outstanding features of his laboratory was his collection of equipment for the testing of blood-blood, which figured in almost every crime case. He had apparatus for testing hemoglobin content, after the method of the late Dr. Zangemeister of Munich, as well as data and material to make the group tests of Beam and Freak.

Sprague's blood, transferred from bandage to a glass slide, went through several tests, each viewed under a microscope.

That blood told a story—a grim story.

And strangely, it brought a fresh memory to the Phantom. He hurried downstairs to the entrance of the loft where there was a big box affixed under a slot in the metal door, like the night-vault box of a bank.

In it Van found a wrapped package. Havens, he knew, had left it here some time previously. He took it upstairs to his desk.

And when he unwrapped the package he was gazing at more maps. All marked "Department of Commerce, U. S." Except for the map which had been made by Havens's staff men-one showing the locales of the Empire and Southwestern Railway sabotage outrages.

Searching through the lot Van found what must have been the original map of the planned airport in Nevada, work on which the scientists had engaged for the Government before resigning their posts.

It was a large map, and property on it was marked off according to ownership. The first words Van saw were: "Empire and Southwest Railway."

So the railroad's right of way ran right through this section of Nevada! It extended out pretty far, too; to the boundary of government-owned property. The airport, however, was planned to be situated some distance away from the railroad.

The Phantom submitted that map to an intensive analysis, using even a violet ray to bring out every detail.

And then he found it!

It had been cleverly done, leaving little trace. But it was there!

Originally, this Government map had been different! The square plot of the airport had, instead of being so removed, actually bordered on the railway's property. The marks designating the original plot had been erased, doubtless by chemicals.

Nodding in sudden understanding, the Phantom rapidly sketched in that original plot. And then, partly across the square but mostly in the railroad property that immediately adjoined it, he wrote a single word-with a question mark after it. The word was:

Pitchblende?

In increasing excitement at his discoveries, he hurriedly viewed the other map showing the locales of the train sabotaging. Yes, most of it had taken place in the Southwest-in Kansas as a matter of fact, where the railway had its biggest Southwestern spurs, and where that streamlined train had been wrecked.

It had also taken place along other points of the many tracks, in other states. But Nevada had been neglected by the saboteurs! Not one spot was marked there.

Thrusting all his deductions temporarily into a recess in his brain to await further analysis, Van turned back to the immediate problem in hand. The exact location of the criminal's Long Island hide-out. He must follow that up. And there was something else, too.

On another table he now dumped out the stuff he had taken from the Piedmont Hotel room. Carefully he went through the collection.

Cigarettes. Currency-wads of crisp new bills. A little loose change; a watch. Keys, and an oblong card on which was printed:

GRAND CENTRAL TERMINAL CHECKROOM
NUMBER 138

It was the last item which most interested the Phantom. What had those thugs left in the depot checkroom? Here was something that warranted immediate investigation.

The Phantom called Police Headquarters, and in a moment was connected with Inspector Gregg.

"Inspector, I suggest you and some of your men meet me in the waiting room of Grand Central Terminal as soon as possible," Van said authoritatively. "I have to look into something there-and I also have some information to convey to you concerning the base from which the Tycoon has been operating in New York."

"What's that?" came the inspector's gruff ejaculation. "I'll be there all right, Phantom!"

Chapter XIX
Another Victim

Good as his word the detective chief was promptly on time. When the Phantom, his features once more disguised, entered the big concourse, stripped now of the waving banners that had given it a festive air, he saw the big, placid-faced inspector and a group of plainclothes men shifting impatiently.

The Phantom identified himself without having to show his badge, since he was expected here.

"Well, now, what's this about the criminal's base of operations?" the inspector demanded at once.

"I hope I haven't stirred up any false hopes, inspector." Van smiled tightly. "My information isn't too definite. And it can wait a little longer. I want you and your men to be on hand now, just in case there's any trouble. Let them spread out a bit, but watch me."

The command was carried out swiftly. Plainclothes men scattered about the concourse, amongst the coming and going travelers.

The Phantom walked straight to the checkroom counter. A uniformed attendant, youthful and sleepy-eyed, waited upon him. Van presented check number 138.

The clerk looked at it, then turned to the row of wire-wickered shelves. He took down a small black valise, shoved it over the counter. Van carried it away carelessly, feeling a sense as of anticlimax.

Inspector Gregg joined the Phantom to walk with him into the adjoining smoking room, which was almost vacant. Other detectives, at Van's command, made a screen around him.

Picking the lock of the valise as it stood on a bench, was a matter of seconds for the Phantom. The lid came open-and a low cry of amazement burst from the inspector, while the Phantom's eyes went to slits.

Stacks of engraved paper lay in the valise. Negotiable stock certificates of the Empire and Southwest Railway!

Hastily pulling on a glove, the inspector was already going through them, his heavy lips pursed as they always were in moments of climax. The Phantom pulled out another paper that laid beneath the stock. On it were cryptic figures-algebraic formulae, a few chemical quantities. And the name inscribed across its top was: "Donald Vaughan."

"Lord, what does this mean, Phantom?" said the puzzled inspector. "Stock placed in a check room? Who —"

"My guess," Van said slowly, "is that Donald Vaughan, the geologist, put it here and gave the check to one of the gang. That's how I got the check-from a dead gangster's room. I think we've uncovered the method of collecting extortion, though, inspector. The checkroom was used as the place of exchange."

"But that would be crazy; imagine using a public checkroom-Say, wait!"

Stirred to action now as the Phantom closed the suitcase, the inspector barked orders to his men.

They went to the checkroom. The sleepy-eyed youth was promptly put through a grilling. He disclaimed any knowledge of what had been going on. He couldn't remember faces, he said, and there were so many people. Van, looking at him, thought he was telling the truth.

Taking matters into his own hands, and dispensing with the formality of procuring a search warrant, the inspector barked orders for the whole checkroom to be searched for more such stuff.

"It beats me!" he told the Phantom. "I still can't understand how anybody would have the nerve to use such a place for his extortion collections."

"Why not?" Van asked, even as a new, vague, but disturbing apprehension began stirring within him. "Isn't it the last place we would have thought of looking? And accessible to anyone? Anybody could safely collect the loot, just as the men who had secretly to pay it could put it there unnoticed. If you ask me it was a most ingenious method. I suggest that you look up Donald Vaughan at once."

"They'll know up at the offices, probably, where to find him," said Gregg confidently, and dispatched a man there. "Well, one thing is sure. They won't be using that checkroom again!" He scowled heavily. "And now, Phantom, what about that information about the base of operations?"

"You can send word to the police in Long Island to search in two areas for a house of this description," Van said, and gave the description.

The inspector concealed his eagerness to be off-this news had evidently interested him more than the discovery of stock-as, on the heels of a plainclothes man, two of the men whom Van had seen in the upstairs office on the night of the tragedy in the concourse, came hurrying to the scene.

James Strickland, the florid-faced vice-president of the Empire and Southwest Railway; and Jenson, the mild, bespectacled secretary of the line.

"What is it now?" Strickland's voice was hoarse, agitated. "We've been here trying to check reports on that streamline train wreck-have our hands full. What's this about Vaughan?"

"Where can we get a hold of him?" It was the inspector who answered, for the Phantom hadn't identified himself to these newcomers.

Strickland was looking from the group of men outside the checkroom to the frightened checkroom clerk. He shook his head, jerkily.

"I don't know just where Vaughan would be at this hour —" he began.

"Why, he must be at his laboratory," Jenson promptly broke in. "He sleeps there when he's working, and he's been working all this week. It's on East Sixteenth Street." He gave the number.

"Okay." A moment later Inspector Gregg, having drawn Van aside, said in a low voice: "I'll send a couple of men there to see Vaughan. Let's take the trail of this Tycoon's base ourselves, and —"

"Let other men attend to that job," Van put in, his tone crisp, incisive. "And you-and plenty of police-come along to Vaughan's at once!"

Something in his tone stopped any protest the inspector might have intended making. He told one of his men to attend to communicating Van's message about the criminals' base to the Long Island authorities.

Minutes later, the inspector's car, in which he rode with the Phantom and several other men, was screaming through the scant night traffic, down and across town. Behind it came two prowl-cars with their bluecoat duos.

On a dark desolate street, in the shadow of tall factory chimneys and where the East River bridges could be seen etched against the sky, the cars with sirens screaming slid to a stop opposite a modern, trim building which looked almost incongruous in this neighborhood.

The Phantom and the police leaped swiftly to the curb, strode to the front door of the building. Van pushed a bell. They could hear it ring inside, but there was no answer.

It was the inspector who seized the handle, turned it. He gave an ejaculation of surprise as he found it unlocked, then yanked the door open and —

The concussion of the sudden, terrific explosion sent the inspector and several of his men flying backward, the Phantom with them! The house shook on its very foundations. Windows shattered! Smoke billowed out the open door.

Before the smoke had cleared, the Phantom, gun out, had leaped ahead of the other men into the house.

Flashlights went on in the hands of police who followed him, illuminating a large, devastated chamber.

It had been a laboratory. Now it was a mess of broken lights.

And then, one and all, the flashlights focused on the debris-strewn floor.

There, horribly mangled, and in a pool of blood, lay the body of Donald Vaughan, geologist.

He had been literally blown in two. The middle of his body was one sagging mass of broken bones and flesh. His squarish face, with its heavily pouched eyes, was distorted and twisted out of shape, blood frothed the purple lips.

The Phantom took in the gruesome sight in a flash and then his eyes roved fiercely about the flashlit room, taking cognizance of wrecked apparatus and particularly of one broken glass tube filled with a peculiar gilt foil.

His glance swept suddenly then to an open door, a corridor in the rear which the darkness there had at first obscured. The only exit.

His lithe body hurtled forward. Out into the corridor, to a rear door, his gun out. He yanked the door open, revealing a rear alley leading to the next block. He stopped abruptly. The dark alley was full of slouch-hatted figures, apparently just making a get-away. This he saw only fleetingly as he opened the door, for in the next instant he had ducked back.

Shots flamed from two directions. Gunmen had seen the door opening and were cutting loose, their guns giving the alarm to the rest.

From behind the door frame the Phantom grimly aimed, and his own gun blazed.

One of the thugs dropped in his tracks, pitched to the paving.

Then, just as the rest started to cut loose with blazing guns, police came pounding to the doorway.

"Get those thugs!" Van yelled. "They're the Tycoon's gang!"

He would never forget the faces of the men he had seen in that plateau experience in the Catskills.

The police leaped out. Shots from steady, flaming Police Positives shattered the night. The alley became a bedlam.

Gangsters fell, their life-blood spurting redly as they paid for trying to shoot it out and resist capture. Others tried to flee up the alley onto the next street, where they evidently had their cars. But police prowl coupes had already sped around to head them off, to blockade the alley.

The Tycoon's gang was caught between two fires. As if they realized that capture meant death, they fought like cornered rats. Two of the police were badly wounded —a bluecoat, writhing on the pavement with a side wound, and a detective hobbling bravely on one wounded leg while he still tried to fire his gun.

The Phantom himself was in the midst of the fray, and again the Nemesis of Crime was taking a grim toll. A face loomed before him in the gun-blazing alley-the twisted face of Maxie. Van took aim, only to see the thug go down before the gun of one of the bluecoats. But at the same instant Van saw another figure only too familiar —a flashy-dressed, dancer-like figure, the scar on his otherwise handsome face showing livid in the night. Slick!

The Phantom leaped forward, gun whipping up as he ducked a desperate shot from the gang lieutenant.

Again, he aimed.

And again he held his fire. For out of the swirling mass of figures, the acrid mist of powder-smoke, leaped a slender shape. Kitty, the gun moll! With a scream, she had leaped in front of the man who, though an underworld felon, was the man she loved.

And though Van knew she was a cold-blooded killer, he could not shoot at that slender shape.

Seeing that, Slick took cruel advantage of it. He grabbed the woman who had furnished him her own body as a shield. He started to retreat, dragging her backward with him; his callous answer to her love.

But evidently one of the zealous bluecoats hadn't seen that she was a woman.

She slumped so suddenly, with a stricken cry, that Slick could not hold her up to longer shield him. Like the cornered rat he was, he flung up his gun, aimed straight for the Phantom. But the Phantom beat him to it. Even as he was sidestepping Slick's bullet that whistled by his ear, the Phantom's own bullet found the cowardly Slick's heart.

As Slick's lifeless body sank to the paving, Van swiftly leaped forward. He caught up the limp, moaning girl, carried her out of the melee to the nearest place of safety. There he lowered her.

One look, even in the darkness, told him that she was beyond help. The bullet had entered too close to her heart.

In a moment she stirred, her eyes flickering; no longer cold, but frightened, like a child's.

"Slick!" she murmured. "Don't let them get you, Slick."

The Phantom leaned close, spoke softly. "Slick's all right," he lied. "They have taken him alive." But then he hardened himself, to take grim advantage of the lie. "Maybe it'll go easier with him if you speak up," he suggested.

"I'll talk," she gasped, even as the death rattle began in her throat. "It ain't his fault —I'm to blame." She too, was lying, and Van knew it. "He's just a baby, honest —"

"You posed as Nurse Keenan." Van forced his words to rap hard against that ebbing consciousness, even as the roar of guns was subsiding in the alley. "But you were also Nancy Clay. Right?"

"Yes."

"The Tycoon got you that job of airplane hostess, too? And you did the trick, didn't you?"

"Yes. I gave —" She broke off, a paroxysm shaking her slender body.

But the Phantom was unrelentingly persistent. He bent closer. "Do you know who the Tycoon is?"

Fear fanned the dying spark in the girl's eyes. "I —I thought I did-heard voice-saw-Guess I was wrong —"

Van leaned still closer. "Who did you think it was? Was it —" Into her ear he spoke a name.

She raised her head a little as if to answer-but before she did, a final paroxysm shook her body. Her eyes went dull, and she lay still.

It was just as well, Van reflected in that gruesome moment. For what he had on her would have doomed her to the chair —

Chapter XX
The Conference

When Van Loan turned from the girl's body, the sweating police were sheathing their smoking guns. They were standing about, looking foolishly idle as men always look immediately after a fray, when there is nothing more to do. Saluting the warriors, the Phantom walked back into the blasted house. "Well, we wiped 'em out!" Back in the shattered laboratory, where emergency lights had been rigged up by a hastily summoned riot squad, Inspector Gregg spoke tersely to the Phantom. "We got them all, thanks to your quickness."

Van's disguised face showed no triumph. Instead, his eyes were thoughtful, sober, and his lithe body, if anything, was more tense than ever.

Homicide men had come, were working about the mangled corpse of Donald Vaughan. The verdict of "death from bombing" pronounced by the stocky medical examiner, however, was superfluous.

"Now if we can only get the Tycoon himself!" the inspector gritted. And the thought sent him to a telephone which by some miracle had been found to be in working order. He called Headquarters.

"Any news from Long Island about that house?" he demanded. His grunt of disappointment was enough. "Okay. Well, keep in touch with them. I'll be at this number for a while."

He hung up. But hardly a minute had passed before the telephone rang insistently.

"Hello!" The inspector was back at the instrument. "What's that? You just got a news flash? Yes, I'll wait." He waited, his face hopeful. "Yes?" He listened, and the hopeful look turned to blank amazement.

With a short exclamation he hung up, turned to the Phantom.

"Listen to this." His gruff voice shook with excitement. "Just when the Long Island police were starting the search of the areas you suggested someone phones them an anonymous tip to go to a certain house in Elmore. They thought it was a crank, but went anyway. And it was the house you described. They raided it-but no one was there. They found that air-conditioned room, you described, though, with a lot of crazy-fangled machinery in it —"

For a moment Van's eyes were puzzled. "But they did learn something, didn't they, inspector?" he demanded.

"I'll say they did." The inspector sprang his climax. "Guess who owns that house. Winston B. Garrison-the railway president who's in the sanitarium. What do you say we interview him-and find out just how cooped up he is? Maybe he's been getting around more than we have thought!"

"Maybe," Van said noncommittally, remembering that murder in the sanitarium, and the faked trip to St. Louis.

And then his eyes gleamed with decision. He turned to the inspector hurriedly.

"Inspector, I'm leaving this case here in your hands for the time being. Do whatever you deem wisest."

"You talk as if you're leaving town." The inspector laughed.

The Phantom moved through the death-room for the door.

"I am," was his parting remark, spoken with grim purpose.

Half an hour later a surprised, haggard-eyed Frank Havens, who had hardly had time to express his relief at seeing Van safe and sound, stared up from his desk in the *Clarion* office.

"I've chartered the plane as you asked, Van," the publisher said. "But I can't understand your bolting off like this again! Leaving this case virtually dangling-just when it seems headed for a finish, with the gang caught —"

"I'm following the trail to that very finish, Frank," the Phantom told him determinedly.

He had been re-packing a bag with clothes he had thrown in hastily at his own apartment. He took out his Colt, snapped back the slide, cleaned and oiled the gun.

"I may be wrong, but something tells me I'm not. The Tycoon no longer has the jump on me. But I know he's not through yet, even with his New York mob wiped out, and unless I work fast —"

The ringing of the phone interrupted him. Havens answered it. He spoke briefly, listened. And his rugged face went suddenly taut with shock.

"That was Inspector Gregg, Van. He said to tell you, if you were still in town, that Garrison has disappeared. He's vanished from that sanitarium. Dr. Ferris is gone, too, And that's not all. The inspector has been unable to contact any of the other men involved. Sprague has left the Polyclinic and has vanished with the rest. It's as if everyone concerned has suddenly disappeared."

Even before Havens finished, Van's whole body felt rippling with impatience. He slammed his suitcase shut, speaking with gripping firmness:

"I expected this, Frank. It confirms everything. I was right when I said I had to work fast."

* * *

The railway depot of the Empire and Southwest's biggest line, a line hard hit by sabotage, was a concrete structure, by no means as imposing as the Grand Central Terminal in New York, but even more modern in its design and equipment.

The large, spacious office on the ground floor was an excellent place for a secret conference. Its windows could be closed as tightly as its door, for the room was air-conditioned, and the air that came through a wall vent was fresh and invigorating.

But the six men who sat around a table in the room seemed uncomfortable, despite this air. Not one who did not look tense, haunted and nerve-ridden.

Winston B. Garrison, his face gaunt, the skin like crumpled parchment, sat at the head of the table. The glass, which had held the morphomine he had just finished, was at his side. Next to him sat his physician, tall, dark-eyed Dr. Ferris.

James Strickland and Jenson came next, the latter busily polishing his glasses.

Then Paul Talbert, the wind-burned, mustached shoring engineer, and the shock-headed Leland Sprague, surveyor. Two scientists where there had originally been eight! And yet the secret bond which had held those eight so close now held these remaining two.

Talbert sat erect, but his eyes were bloodshot. Sprague was squirming uneasily, his lips twitching strangely from time to time.

"Well —" Strickland spoke, a little hoarsely. "Well, here we are, after two days in that train we had to run out so secretly!" He glanced at Garrison. "If you ask me this trip was foolish. What can we accomplish here?"

Garrison strained forward. "I've got to salvage my railway." His voice was a hoarse croak, but there was determination in it. "Though our lines have been virtually ruined, I was informed, from here, that the sabotaging has stopped since the wreck of the streamlined train. We've got to work out a plan! A plan!"

"Don't excite yourself, Mr. Garrison," Dr. Ferris said soothingly. "Just take it easy, and keep taking that medicine —"

"Maybe that medicine isn't doing him so much good," Talbert clipped, pointedly.

The doctor's dark eyes flashed. "Meaning —"

And of a sudden the room seemed to crackle with tension. Eyes clashed-eyes of suspicion and hostility.

Jenson laughed nervously, replacing his glasses.

"Now gentlemen, let's not start accusing each other. We've got to cooperate. The railway —"

"Damn the railway!" Sprague burst out shrilly, "I'm sorry I ever had anything to do with the railway." He laughed wildly. "If it weren't for the others —"

Talbert whirled on him. "Careful, Sprague. You don't know what you're saying. You know all of us, even when a murderer and extortioner was killing off our numbers, kept doing our jobs. We all tried to help Mr. Garrison put the railroad on its feet."

"Did you?" a new, crisp voice asked.

The group at the table whirled as if every head was jerked by strings, cries of alarm coming from several throats in unison. They had not heard the door open.

They gaped as a tall man in a black silk domino mask strode purposefully into the air-conditioned room-followed by four of the city's police.

The Phantom quietly closed the door.

"Keep your seats, gentlemen," he told the group. "I'm the Phantom, and I've come to get to the bottom of this whole ghastly intrigue."

Garrison looked as if he were going to have another of his spells. "But how-where —"

"You wonder at my opportune arrival?" The Phantom smiled grimly beneath his domino mask. "As a matter of fact, I preceded you down here by a full day. I've been waiting for you, and it was easy, with the help of the excellent police here, to check your arrival, and your meeting here."

"What do you want?" Garrison was still spokesman for the startled group. "Why have you brought in those policemen?"

"Largely to prevent any further crimes," the Phantom replied, with a grim smile. "To help me, if I need help, in stopping the Tycoon, once and for all."

Strickland gave a horrified gasp. "What? Then he is down here? He's followed us! God, he'll kill us all!"

"I'm here to stop him," said the Phantom. "And that's why I want to get at the truth. I asked a question when I came in this room —" His eyes swiveled to Talbert. "You were saying how you and the others wanted to help the railroad get on its feet. I challenged that statement."

Talbert's mustache bristled. "What do you mean by that, Phantom? We've all worked like slaves for the railroad. It was to our own monetary interest to make the stock we owned rise in value."

The Phantom made an impatient gesture. "I said it was time for the truth. Wherever there is a big crime like this, I've invariably found that a smaller crime is behind it. Or perhaps you scientists didn't consider it a crime to tamper with a Government map? Or to move the location of a Government field?"

Sprague gave a stricken cry. Talbert sat frozen, now, eyes cold with fear.

"You were men of science, but you were human-too human," the Phantom pursued, relentlessly. "Greed was behind that tampering. Greed made you move the field from the place you had first selected; made you do it so secretly that no one but yourselves knew that it was not the original site. Then it made you resign your Government posts and cleverly induce the Empire and Southwest Railway to take you on as technicians, in return for stock.

"You scientists had been selected by the Government to plan that airport and select its site because of your specialized knowledge. You, Talbert, because you know waterways; Sprague as an expert surveyor, Vaughan for his knowledge of geology, of rock formation; and so on. But when you got actually to work on the original plan of that airport, had selected the site, you unexpectedly came upon some rich deposits of pitchblende. Some of it was on Government property, but most of it was on the property of the Empire and Southwest Railway. Pitchblende! The ore from which the most valuable element in the world is extracted. *Radium!*"

Garrison half rose from his chair, eyes bulging. Strickland and Jenson gaped, and Dr. Ferris sat looking on like a confused observer. Which he was, in truth.

"Radium!" the Phantom repeated. "A word which signifies millions of dollars! A fortune for scientists who had hitherto made only a modest living. But their first fear was that it would be found before they could swing some deal which would give them a grasp on the pitchblende property. If the airport were built on that particular site, because some of the pitchblende was on Government ground, you would have to 'discover' it openly. So, to divert this possibility, you group of scientists, and there were eight of you then —" His gaze was bent on the two at the table. "—changed the Government map. As trusted Government men you had access to the Department of Commerce files, and could accomplish that.

"Then you went to Garrison, to swing the deal that would give you stock in the railway. And through that stock, partial ownership of the property—"

Garrison broke in then, his voice a hoarse croak.

"But they told me nothing of the radium! What I have said about their promise to modernize the line is true-that's why I gave them stock! No wonder they wanted it!" His nervous agitation was gripping him as he singled out one man. "Strickland! What did you know of all this?"

Strickland denied any knowledge. So did Jenson.

The Phantom's eyes were inexorable, seen through the holes of his mask. "The criminal who calls himself the Tycoon *did* know about that radium!" he said flatly. "It was the motivation for his crimes! It was the goal toward which his greed drove him, which led him to murder, to extortion, to sabotage! Radium! That was what the Tycoon was after."

Garrison rose totteringly from his place. "This-this is all-too much of a shock!" he croaked. He seemed like a drunken man. "I—I must beg to be excused. I—I have an errand—"

The police glanced at the Phantom, but he gave no sign, though his eyes had narrowed. And Garrison was permitted to leave the room.

Over his own doctor's protests he went out, closing the door.

The Phantom's glance swiveled to Talbert and Sprague, who had listened speechlessly to his accusations.

"Well, gentlemen. Have you anything to say?"

Sprague's wild eyes looked about. Talbert's tall, strong frame slumped a little. His voice came hoarsely, brokenly.

"What you have said is true, Phantom. I admit my complicity. All of us swung the deal with the railroad to get our fingers on that land. I helped change the map. But-but I swear I had nothing to do with the crimes that have now happened! I swear—"

A strange, groggy sound had come into his voice suddenly, as if he were talking in a daze. Looking about the table, Van saw that the faces of the others were going strangely weary.

Then his own superior physique felt it, and his heart went suddenly icy.

Something invisible was closing upon this room. And then his nostrils detected a faint odor in the air, like that of fresh peaches!

His eyes flashed to the vent through which the conditioned air was coming, the only inlet.

He whirled to the paling police.

"Get everybody out of here! Hurry! And close the door behind them!"

As he spoke he was jerking the door open. Without waiting for the rest, he dashed out into the corridor of the station. The vent! He saw the piping-saw where it curved downward.

His lithe body hurled to a stairway leading to the basement, as he whipped out his Colt. In seconds he was down the stairs on soft-soled shoes, and the darkness of the cellar engulfed him. The lights were not on, but he could hear the whir of an air-conditioning plant.

Then, as his eyes accustomed themselves to the gloom, a shadowy figure leaped toward him with a wild animal-like cry.

Hands like talons clutched at the Phantom before he could aim his gun.

His antagonist was possessed of the strength of desperation.

But the Phantom, his own muscles flexing with the strength of rage, had his left arm free. His jabbing fist found the face in the dark-struck twice. Short, crunching blows.

Chapter XXI
The Dream of Power

Leaping to answer the Phantom's summons the police, followed by the whole group from the executive room who came rushing down to the cellar, found a strange, grim tableau.

The cellar lights were now on but the big air-conditioning plant had been turned off. Close by that plant stood a metal container-small, green-painted, a faint wisp of cloudy stuff emanating from it.

And several feet away, holding a half limp figure in a viselike grip stood the Phantom.

He spoke more with wearied relief than with triumph.

"Here," he said, "is the Tycoon."

The police guns promptly whipped up. Men gave one concerted hoarse cry of astonishment.

"Then it's Garrison!" Strickland yelled. "He left the room just before that gas came in! He came down here!"

"Right!" the Phantom clipped. "He did come down here! And there he is!"

He stepped aside, pulling his prisoner with him. On the floor, just coming to, was the railway president, cruel finger welts on his neck standing out bluely. Dazedly Strickland got to his feet.

"Then who is —" Jenson cried, staring at the man whom the Phantom held in that grip of iron.

Van stepped aside from his prisoner.

Police guns were covering the fellow now.

Every eye was staring at the man, bewildered, as they took in the gaunt body, the thin-haired head, the pallid face covered with thick, dark stubble, and the eyes that glared like live coals.

"Yes, gentlemen," Van's voice rang out, "this is the dreaded Tycoon. Otherwise known to you as-David Truesdale!"

Cries of amazed incredulity rose in protesting chorus.

"But it can't be Truesdale!" Talbert's hysterical cry rose above the tumult. "Truesdale's body was found in the airplane wreck!"

But Jenson, stepping closer to the prisoner, broke out with even greater vehemence: "It *is!* The Phantom is right! It's Truesdale! That beard can't conceal his face!"

"Truesdale!" Sprague screamed shrilly. "So it was you-you who were making me come at your beck-to your hideout-to —"

The glaring prisoner spoke then, his voice thick.

"This is all some mistake! I never heard of any Truesdale. I can identify myself. A mistake —"

"You made the mistake when you first gave yourself away to me, even though I had never seen you," the Phantom said flatly. "The game is up, Truesdale. Your ego-maniacal dream of power is ended. While you were stunned I found enough incriminating papers in your pockets to prove plenty." He handed one paper over to the police. "This list of names and hideout locations," he said, "will finish the mob you had working in this town and state. Just as your mob in New York was finished."

The prisoner's face drained of its last drop of blood. His dark eyes glared wildly.

"All right!" he shrilled. "You found me, Phantom! I knew you were on my trail throughout-knew that only you might ferret me out! I killed them-all of them! *And I'm not through yet!"*

Only a man fired by utter, animal desperation could have moved so swiftly, so unexpectedly.

Before anyone could stop him, David Truesdale, with a maniacal scream, made one mighty leap toward that green-painted metal cylinder.

He lifted it, his hand on the cap, his face like that of some satanic gargoyle.

Whether he intended to hurl it out at the whole group, with its content billowing out, or whether he intended to erase himself as well as the rest, could never have been told-for Van's gun barked then, aiming at the hand unscrewing that cap.

The hand let go as blood spurted from it. The other arm of the criminal still hugged the cylinder, as he cursed and screamed in pain. Then suddenly a horrible change came over him.

His body seemed literally to wither. His distorted face turned greenish. The life went out of his eyes as he slumped slowly to the floor.

Grimly the Phantom swung to the petrified group of men.

"Clear out of here-out into the air! That tube is still leaking! It can't harm you as long as you're not near it-but you can see what one whiff of it, full strength, has done to the devil who brought it here! The Tycoon is dead!"

* * *

"And so it was Truesdale, Van! But I still can't quite grasp the whole fiendish business!"

Frank Havens uttered those words of bewilderment as, two days later, he sat beside Richard Curtis Van Loan in one of the latter's purring touring cars which Van was driving uptown through Manhattan.

"Truesdale was after that radium, Frank," Van said. "Where the others had been content merely to get a share of the property, Truesdale was greedy enough to want all of it! A peculiar man, Truesdale. To his friends he seemed shy, meek. Actually he had a gigantic ego, a terrific greed for power and wealth. And so he planned his devilish crimes-planned them with all the thoroughness of a true scientist.

"His purpose was twofold. He meant to get possession of the stock from the other scientists who knew of the stuff, then to seal their lips. His second aim was to buy what stock he couldn't get by extortion, and this he could do if he lowered its value sufficiently, made it worthless to its holders. His sabotage was inaugurated in an effort to ruin the railway, in the belief that Garrison would finally be glad to sell out, provided he didn't know about that radium. And, since the other scientists had not yet told the president of the Empire and Southwest Railway, killing them would safeguard that secret. Once the murders began, the other scientists dared not talk anyway, for fear their whole intrigue with the Government map would come out.

"Truesdale planned to die-in the eyes of the world. He would be mourned as a victim of the criminal who already had been exploiting himself as the Tycoon. Later on Truesdale could assume a new identity. I believe now that he meant to use Leland Sprague as a sort of inter-mediary-to buy up the depreciating stock for him and do other such work.

"When I learned, from Sprague's shoes, that he had been to the Tycoon's hideout, at first I was suspicious of *him*. But later, I learned the truth. Sprague's blood showed that he had radium poisoning, had evidently contracted it during the experiments conducted at the site of the pitchblende deposits. And he was a cocaine addict. This, which your physician told me, was also confirmed by his blood. Truesdale gave Sprague that cocaine, playing on his illness, converting him to a drug addict so that he would have a man he could use as a slave.

"But to get back to the beginning of Truesdale's crimes. As I said he started them with sabotage of the railway, as soon as he and the others had acquired stock. His first mob —a mob led by Frenchy-operated in Kansas. The money they took from the wrecked trains paid them, and helped pay the second mob Truesdale organized in New York, with Slick as its lieutenant.

"Truesdale knew he must start his murders of the scientists-with himself apparently among the murdered-when he learned they were planning to tell Strickland and Jenson about the radium, after which it would be told to Garrison, who was then supposedly in St. Louis. They had all shrewdly figured that Garrison might react unpleasantly when they told him the real reason they had come into the railway. For Garrison was more interested in the railroad than in anything else. The idea was to tell Strickland and Jenson first, let them in on the fact that all would become rich by exploiting the radium land. With a solid majority they could win Garrison over.

"Truesdale, however, didn't want even Strickland and Jenson to be told the secret. The less who knew about it, the more chance he had of acquiring the stock.

"And Truesdale knew well enough that Garrison wasn't in St. Louis. For in organizing his New York mob, he had been fortunate to get the services of Slick's gun moll, Kitty, a female Jekyll-and-Hyde who had already built up a respectable role for herself as 'Shirley Keenan,' registered nurse. She was well-educated, clever-and I still wonder whether she would have gone wrong if she hadn't fallen for a rat like Slick.

"Garrison, ill from his worries over his failing railroad, was looking for a private nurse, and Truesdale knew it. The gun moll went for the job, got it. This enabled Truesdale to keep tabs on Garrison's movements.

"He learned that Garrison had ordered a big portion of his own stock from vaults in Chicago to be sent to New York. Garrison had already turned over most of the stock he had on hand to the group of scientists. The stock was to come by plane on the maiden flight of the new Harvey airliner.

"I don't know just how Kitty managed to get the job as stewardess, under the name of 'Nancy Clay,' on that airplane. But since Truesdale knew in advance about the flight and the stock order-from her spy work-she had plenty of time to apply for the job, and I believe she got it on her own abilities.

"Meanwhile, Truesdale saw his opportunity to accomplish even more during this airplane flight. He and Garth had gone out West to bring back some of the pitchblende to show the railway officials and convince them. They had the ore in a fireproof briefcase. Later I found a piece of it that Truesdale had failed to remove. That was what first gave me the hint that radium was mixed up in the whole ghastly business.

"With Garth and Truesdale taking the plane from Chicago for the final lap to New York, Truesdale was at last ready to launch his terrible crimes! He began to phone warnings to the other men, demanding both their stock and whatever papers on the pitchblende were in their possession. I found one such paper in Vaughan's satchel full of the stock.

"Truesdale pretended to receive the warnings himself. He acted terrified, his real purport being to spread a contagion of hysteria to the others, so they would meet his demands.

"And now he was ready. In their operations, the gang Truesdale had painstakingly built up used a plane of their own. They had a secret field in the Catskills, where that shack and radio were located.

"Having learned that Pat Bentley was to pilot the Chicago transport, Truesdale got hold of that *Hindenburg* record. Though how he knew of its existence only he could have told. We will never know more, but that's inconsequential.

"On the plane, the gun moll stewardess served drugged coffee to the passengers. Truesdale had not told her he was her boss, though as the Tycoon who knew what was coming, he knew he could insure his own safety. He could only pretend to drink the coffee. However, the girl overheard him talking to Garth. She thought she recognized his voice as that of the Tycoon, but even when she was dying and told me this, she said she wasn't sure.

"Some other member of the gang must have been a stowaway on that plane, for the girl needed help, and all the others aboard are accounted for. When the passengers were drugged, Truesdale also feigning to be drugged with them, the girl and the gangster who aided her cripple the radio, held up the pilot and co-pilot, and made them land on the plateau.

"The rest of that story you know. Three persons who should have been among the dead were missing, you remember. One was Bentley, one the stewardess, and the other, I assumed, was Garth. It was Garth I first suspected up on that plateau, especially since I had found a check of his for twenty-five thousand on the dead Joseph Ware. Now I realize that Ware was frightened and had sold out his stock to Garth, who made the check payable in advance. But to get back, I first accepted the corpse bearing the ring of Truesdale as Truesdale's.

"But by his own move, executed through his gang, Truesdale virtually gave himself away to me. I was to be burned and placed among the dead, to be identified as Bentley, the pilot, by the simple device of putting Bentley's identifications on my charred body. One thing I have learned about even the best criminal minds. That is that they tend to repeat themselves. It occurred to me then that if *my* body could be substituted for Bentley's, then another corpse-and the name of Garth came to me instantly-could be identified as Truesdale's by the same trick.

"But to follow Truesdale. With the plane down, he rushed to New York. Undercover he entered Grand Central Terminal and planted that bomb in the box which motivated the sign, also changing the strip so that it would flash his warning boasts. When the lights flashed, Vincent Brooks and John Eldridge went to investigate the box. The criminal probably counted on Brooks going there, since he was the inventor of the sign. The fact that two went was all the better for Truesdale's plans. When Brooks opened the box, the bomb went off, doing its work on two of the scientists the criminal planned to eliminate.

"Whether Truesdale was anywhere about when I had my set-to with his thugs in the terminal, I don't know. But it is certain he ordered them to follow Bentley and kill him. They were not expecting trouble in making their get-away without going through the gates. I appeared on the scene almost in time to stop that, but they did get away-then.

"Next came the murder of Joseph Ware, at the sanitarium. Ware, I believe, had found out that Garrison was there and not in St. Louis. No doubt he had gone to the sanitarium to tell Garrison the true story about the radium. But Truesdale followed him, killed him and escaped, while the gun moll, Kitty, now posing as Nurse Keenan, cleverly drew my suspicion to Garrison himself, by making it obvious he could have committed the crime. Garrison said later that he had dressed at her suggestion, that it would be good for him. But he had been too confused at the time to tell me that. Naturally she must have seen Truesdale then, too, but quite as naturally, not in his real character. Truesdale also was something of an adept at disguise.

"Fastening suspicion on Garrison was a part of Truesdale's scheme. The disgrace would help to further cripple the railway, lower the buying price of what stock he could not extort.

"Next, Truesdale learned that the airplane wreck had been found. He was not ready for it to be found. As I told you previously, he thought he had plenty of time to clear up that scene, to remove all possible clues, so his 'body' could be neatly found when he tipped off searching parties.

"He sent his gang there in a hurry, but I got there first. You know what happened there.

"When learning that the moll and the nurse were one and the same, I got into the shoes of Frenchy. I learned that the criminal had an active mob in the Southwest. It was they who wrecked the streamlined train in Kansas. Though Truesdale had planned to have it wrecked by being bombed from the plane I was on as 'Frenchy,' he was taking no chances of a slip-up, and his other men were on the job.

"Back at my laboratory I found how the scientists had altered the Government map you got for me. I had already analyzed the little piece of pitchblende, and the evidence of radium poisoning in Sprague's blood gave me final corroboration. From the other map, showing locations of the sabotage activity, I saw that one area in Nevada was untouched; also that the center of sabotage activity was Kansas. Where I had myself seen the vandalism at its worst.

"Now came the checkroom business, and the discovery of the extortion method, followed by Vaughan's murder. In the dead geologist's laboratory I saw shattered parts of an electroscope. I realized then that Vaughan had probably been making radium tests, and the bomb had been used as much to shatter his work as to kill him.

"But the gang who had committed this murder and who had destroyed the laboratory was trapped. They were cleaned up. The Tycoon must quickly have learned this, and realized that without his gang, operations in New York were temporarily at a standstill. So he tipped off the police about the house in Elmore, Long Island, for which I had already started them looking.

"The house proved to be Garrison's, making him the leading police suspect, which was what Truesdale wanted. Actually Garrison had not occupied it for years. Truesdale had rented it and had converted it into a hide-out, with the air-conditioned room. As you know, he was an expert at ventilating.

"From all this I deduced that Truesdale would now have to go out to the Southwest, where he had his other mob, if he wanted to continue operations. Nor was I surprised when it was reported that Garrison and the rest had 'vanished.' Truesdale had managed somehow to get word to Garrison that the sabotaging in Kansas had stopped, and that there now was a chance to repair the damage. So Garrison and the rest left for Topeka.

"When the meeting took place in Garrison's Topeka office, Truesdale was down at the air-conditioner, having knocked out the engineer. Through a vent he could overhear what was taking place in the room. When he heard me revealing the whole background of the crime he started mixing chlorine gas with the air.

"Garrison must have detected it, and thinking something wrong with the vent, gone down to investigate. Truesdale knocked him out, too. But by that time I had become aware of the gas and had hurried down to the cellar myself."

The phantom was slowing the car near Havens's apartment hotel. "And there's the whole thing, Frank," he said. "I still feel that it was Pat Bentley, bringing it to my doorstep, who helped most in its solution."

Havens sat back, a smile of heartfelt relief on his face.

"You've done a wonderful job, Van," he commented. "Bentley did not die in vain."

The car drew nearer to the curb when a girl's voice called a cheery greeting. Muriel Havens came across the pavement.

"Dad! And you, Van! Where have you been, stranger?"

"Hop in," Van invited, "and I'll tell you all about it."

Havens took the wheel then. Van and Muriel sat in the back. And somehow with Muriel beside him, Van forgot his fatigue, and how wearied was his brain that was still teeming with details of the ghastly affair his skill had brought to a solution.

"I've been sleeping most of the time," he drawled to Muriel. "You know, one gets bored."

But though his tone was the languid, idle tone which Muriel so despised, she felt his strong hand close over hers, taking it with brief but warm possession.

Yes, brief. For sooner or later, another baffling crime must break-and again Richard Van Loan would have to forget all human, all personal feelings, and hurl his energy and skill against a diabolical criminal.

www.ingramcontent.com/pod-product-compliance
Lightning Source LLC
Chambersburg PA
CBHW071341130626
46556CB00004B/1969